PLAYING
on Higher
GROUND

Book Two in the *High Ground* Series

Max -
To my best friend
who's always encouraged me
+ supported me throughout life.
You are simply as good as
they come. Thankful 4 you.

RAY SANTIAGO III

²⁰ My son, pay attention to what I say;
turn your ear to my words.
²¹ Do not let them out of your sight,
keep them within your heart;
²² for they are life to those who
find them and health to one's whole body.
²³ Above all else, guard your heart,
for everything you do flows from it.
Proverbs 4:20-23 NIV

Moyer wasn't getting it. "Are you aware of how you talk about yourself?" Dorfman asked. "It's all negative. 'I can't, I can't, I can't,' I've seen your act, kid, and you need to get better. You need to change your thinking. Your process needs to be positive. You have to train yourself to hear a negative thought, stop, let it run its course, and then let it go. 'Cause it doesn't mean crap. The only thing that matters is focusing on the task at hand, which is making that pitch. The task at hand."
— Sport Psychologist Harvey Dorfman
to MLB Pitcher Jamie Moyer,
Just Tell Me I Can't, pg. 20

PLAYING ON HIGHER GROUND

Chapter 01

FRIDAY, SEPTEMBER 13, 2019, 6:49 A.M.

1st Weight Room Session,
Orange Coast College, Costa Mesa, California

I DROP TO A KNEE, scavenging for air that's not coming. Sweat escapes my headband onto the 50-pound kettlebell.

Get up, Jacoby.

My legs don't listen. Ten feet away, my roommate, Tim Fletcher, gets ready to back squat 300 pounds, no problem. *What I'd do for a bit of that. And a bit of his girlfriend.* The thought of her mocha skin and light blue eyes sitting across from me in statistics steals away the pain momentarily.

Sarge, our strength coach, is on the prowl. "Hands off your knees, gentlemen!" His words shock life back into my legs.

"I can smell last night's vodka oozing from your pores. I know you underage angels would never drink the night before early morning workouts. Ten seconds 'til last round."

No time to chalk up. I eyeball the slick kettlebell handle, then the floor-to-ceiling mirror in front of me that's misted over.

"Last round!" Sarge's voice echoes off the mirrors. "Ninth inning. Ready . . . go."

My trembling fingers grip the dead weight. Using my hips to gain power in my torso, I repeatedly thrust the heavy kettlebell overhead like an intoxicated sports fan attempting the wave. I can't tell who's in charge—the kettlebell or me.

"Thirty seconds left!" Sarge struts closer until his cinnamon breath invades my personal space, stinging my nostrils. "Johnson, you best squeeze that brimming bowl of Jell-O you call a backside at the top of that swing."

"Yes, Coach."

"I heard about you. Nineteen-year-old, medical redshirt freshman. Shoulda been a first-round draft pick outta high school 'til you blew out your elbow. Then lost your D-1 scholly. Tragic. Don't go thinking you'll be handed a spot here just because it's junior college baseball. SoCal JUCO ball's no joke. You hear me, bonus baby?"

"Not looking . . . for handouts . . . Coach," I mutter through gritted teeth. *A little personal space would be nice, though.*

"It'll take a lot more than 94-mile-an-hour talent to get drafted," Sarge continues. "But if you hang with me, I'll have you throwing 96 by spring if you don't throw up on me first."

His words give my stomach a bad idea.

"Everything you got, gentlemen. No one will out work you. Maybe tomorrow, but not today. Not right now."

The kettlebell is slipping through my failing fingers. With each heave, my Apple Watch meets me at eye level, blinking 171 bpm, but I don't need technology to tell me I'm about to pass out. On the next upswing, my black rubber bracelet sends me a nice reminder, *Phil 4:13*: *I can do all things through Him who strengthens me.*

You and me, God. You and me.

"Ten seconds, gentlemen! Fight or fold. Your choice."

Fight. *Six seconds. The draft . . . five seconds . . . millions . . . four seconds . . . San Diego beachfront . . . three seconds . . . girls . . . two seconds . . . almost there . . . one second . . . victory.*

"And relax."

My two favorite words slide from Sarge's mouth. Barbells collide with weight racks as kettlebells, med balls, and bodies thud the black mats, mine included.

"Get up," Sarge barks. "Never let fatigue know you're tired."

We climb to our feet like elderly men ready to take on the early-bird special at Denny's. I look back. My sweat shadow still lay out cold on the mat next to the kettlebell.

"Good work, gentlemen."

I know that tone. We're not done. Sure enough, Sarge sets out 45-pound cement plates around the gym. His dark chiseled arms turn them into three-pound feathers. "Grab some water and meet me back here in one minute."

My Hydro Flask is drained after two gulps before my lungs demand more air. Around the gym there are more eyes on me than necessary, sizing up my million-dollar arm, I'm sure. Nothing new. Prior to the 2018 Major League Baseball draft, and before my injury, I'd gained enough hype and popularity that they—whoever *they* is—gave me one of those little blue checkmarks next to my name on Instagram and Twitter. I wish they hadn't.

"Grab your girlfriends." Sarge signals to the cement plates leaning against the walls. The sophomores gravitate toward them but their body language is running for the exits. They know what's coming. I don't care to find out. Sarge grabs a 45-pound plate and thrusts it overhead.

"You can walk around, stand still, sing a song, or imagine your real girlfriend weighs only three of these plates instead of six—I don't care. Your only job is to keep it locked out above-head for two minutes. I promise you this'll be more mental than physical. Your mind's about to whisper lies to you, then scream them. Go somewhere else. Hawaii, Jamaica, Antarctica . . . I don't care. Just don't give into the pain."

Sarge's words remind me of a warning Mack, my sport psychologist, issued me about the dangers of listening to my thoughts when my heart rate's above 150 bpm. He says my thoughts will tell me anything I want to hear, just to relieve the discomfort. Mack wasn't lying. Right now, nothing sounds better than throwing in the towel on a-year-and-a-half of physical therapy, slapping my sling back on, grabbing a pizza, and living out my days binge-watching Michael Scott manage *The Office*.

"Anyone drops their weight fails themselves and every guy on this team," Sarge says. "You succeed or fail on your own, but you win or lose as one. My suggestion . . . sophomores?"

"Don't be that guy," they yell on cue.

We thrust our 'girlfriends' overhead. My fingers fight mine as she's already squirming to be put down.

"Two minutes, gentlemen," Sarge shouts. "Ready, go!"

A thin crack in the rubber mat whisks me and my 45-pound plate off on a winding trail to next year, nine months from now: June 1, 2020, in New York City—well, nearby Secaucus, New Jersey, where the Major League Baseball draft is held every year at the MLB Network studios. I'm wearing a shimmering gray suit, sitting alongside my parents and several of the best amateur baseball players in the country, staring up at a podium in front of a giant green draft board, ready to make us millionaires with one signature.

The Baseball Commissioner approaches the podium, adjusts the mic, opens an envelope, and pauses over the crowd, "With the first overall pick of the 2020 Major League Baseball Draft, the Detroit Tigers select Jacoby Johnson of Orange Coast College, Costa Mesa, California."

"One minute down!" Sarge's words drag me back to the gym.

"Stay up stay strong!"

The crack in the rubber mat now leads me back to the mirror where 30 minutes ago I scribbled 6/1/20 in the mist for this exact moment—the moment my shoulders fail, my elbows sting, my back spasms, my glutes cease to fire, and my eyelids sting with sweat or tears, or both. Every ounce of me screaming, pleading, tempting me to give in.

Drop her.

But *6/1/20* won't let me. Not yet, at least. *It's me and you, God.*

"Thirty seconds!"

Around the gym, grunts grow louder from teammates' swaying back and forth holding up their 45-pound plates like nests in the wind. Gravity presses harder into mine.

Go back to draft day.

Posing with the Commissioner for pictures in my white button up Tigers jersey over my shirt and tie and donning a navy blue baseball cap with the classic Detroit "D." In the crowd, Mom and Dad are standing next to each other, even if just for me. Mom's hands are clasped at her mouth fighting back tears, and Dad's hands are behind him as he rocks on his feet, proud of me and the journey we started in T-ball.

But gravity is winning.

"Johnson, you better get that weight off your head and straighten that back or we'll start this all over again. No special privileges here, pretty boy."

I've never asked for special privileges. I bend my knees and jump a bit to thrust my girlfriend back overhead. I call for help from my glutes, but they abandoned me long ago. I can't. Seconds before the two minutes are up, my plate pounds the mat.

"Is that you back there, Johnson?"

A steady stream of sweat drips to my cement plate. "Yes, Coach."

"You know what that means, gentlemen. Go grab water. We'll try this again. You can thank the bonus baby."

One by one, thirsty zombies shoulder past me, mumbling their disgust. I can't blame them. My eyes never leave my girlfriend. Then, Shawn Bauer, our sophomore starting catcher, wraps a greasy arm around me. "It's alright, big guy. Girls will get the best of you sometimes. I've been that guy, too."

Thirty seconds later, I'm swaying next to Sarge as the team encircles us, girlfriends in hand for another two-minute twirl. The only thing worse than joining them is having to watch.

"Ready." Everyone raises their plates overhead. I lower my eyes to avoid their daggers. "At ease, gentlemen."

Around the weight room, 45-pounders pummel the rubber flooring as Sarge puts up a hand to hush the guys. "You have Shawn Bauer to thank. Each one of you walked by Jacoby and not a single guy offered any encouragement—except him. He literally took him under his wing—which right about now is the nastiest place in Orange County—and built him up."

Everyone summons the strength to laugh. I leave my girlfriend's gaze just long enough to steal a peek at Bauer and nod.

"*That* is more valuable than any extra work," Sarge says. "Remember this moment. When a teammate is down, no matter if you're a potential big leaguer or just here for the Big League Chew bubble gum, any one of you have the ability—heck, the responsibility—to lift each other up. Especially you sophomores. Tim, why do we come in here?"

"To get stronger, Coach."

"Why do we get stronger?"

"So we can perform better."

"And how do we get stronger?"

"By lifting weights."

"What's another name for weight?"

"Pounds?"

Everyone but me laughs again.

"Nice try." Sarge picks up my cement plate and holds it like a waiter carrying a pizza to a table. The chatter dies down. "Weight is stress. It's a demand imposed on the body. And when your resources, your muscles, aren't strong enough to withstand the demand"—he lowers the plate and turns to me—"what happens, Johnson?"

"You fail."

"Exactly."

Sarge turns to address the team that's now taking a wobbly knee, leaving me as the last one standing. And not in the good way. He raises the weight back above head. "But, as you get stronger, and resist the temptation to give in, trust me guys, you never regret it. Finishing strong is the truest test of strength. The real reward."

I slink to join the team on a knee even though lying on my back with eyes closed and an oxygen mask sounds better.

"The weight doesn't change, gentlemen. Your resources do. Your muscles do. They grow. And allow you to do more. Handle more. Become more. Then what do we do, Bauer?"

"Add more weight, Coach."

"We add more weight." He stacks a second 45-pounder on the first and holds both above head one-handed without a grimace. "You don't grow stronger unless you overcome greater demand. In here, we increase the weight on purpose, for a purpose. Out there"—he gestures towards the door with his free hand— "the weight, the stress, the demands of life and sport will find you and it'll be up to you to increase your resources, whether it be family, friends, faith, or whatever, to meet the demands life throws at you."

I tug at my Philippians 4:13 bracelet without breaking eye contact. Suddenly, a cramp in my lower back threatens to bite before my fist discreetly punches it away. I don't need any more negative attention.

"You'll be competing with and against each other for the next eight weeks of Fall Ball to prove you belong in the starting lineup come spring. But who will be your greatest opponent?"

"You," Bauer shouts.

Laughter forces Sarge to bring the weights down to the ground. When I see him chuckling, I join in, too. When the noise subsides, Sarge searches the room for a pair of bold eyes. "Besides me, who will be your greatest opponent?"

"Ourselves," I say, meeting his gaze.

"That's right, Johnson. Everyone take a look around." Bodies on one knee all perk up. "Some of you won't make it through Fall Ball. Coach Hill, Coach Jenkins and I see it every year. There's pressures and pleasures around every corner pulling you away from the one place you're all hopefully working toward, which is what sophomores?"

"Fresno." They sit up even straighter, chests out, while still trained on Sarge. "You best know that everyone in the state is gunning for you guys. We accomplished something special last year in winning state for the fourth time in the last 10 years. But that's in the past now. We don't get to May without today."

Sarge drags a cardboard box to the middle of the circle and holds out a bright orange T-shirt. On the backside, in navy blue lettering, it says *MAY starts with TODAY*. He tosses the T-shirts toward us, sparking refreshed chatter. "It's a daily grind, gentlemen. That's why every *today* matters. Make them count. Get a break and get out of here."

7:04 A.M.

Outside the weight room, my lungs and legs are still recovering as the sun begins its daily climb. Mack's steadying voice chimes in: *When you control your breathing, you control your body, when you control your body, you control your performance. It all starts with the deep breath.*

My nostrils soak in the pure air no longer mixed with body odor and vodka. *Inhale...2...3...4...hold...2...3...4...exhale... 2...3...4...empty...2...3...4.* I repeat this several times before the weight room door swings open and Sarge's paw gives me a drenched pat on the back.

"You don't have to like the workouts." He points towards the baseball field in the distance where morning dew still blankets the infield turf and clay mound. "You just have to love what they allow you to do out there."

A radar gun flashing 96 mph runs through my mind.

We continue to stare out at the field when he asks, "How'd the elbow feel today? Tommy John's no joke."

"It felt all right. It's the rest of me that hurts."

"That's just day one." Sarge flashes his Crest White smile. "Listen, I put you on blast in front of everyone, not to embarrass you, but to send a message. Every guy in there thinks he should be D-1 or in pro ball. But they're here"—he lifts his Oakley's, revealing his honey browns—"and *you're* here. Even if you feel you might belong somewhere else. You've got a target on your back with those guys on and off the field. They either want to be you or beat you."

"I know. Comes with the territory."

"I guess. You throwing this weekend?"

"Tomorrow. All fastballs 'til I'm cleared to throw off-speed."

"How long's it been?"

My elbow pulses at the memory of walking off the mound with the trainer after the sharp snap in my elbow, effectively ending my high school career and the possibility of being picked in the 2018 draft. My gaze returns to the field. "May 18th, 2018. That's the last time I threw in a game. Sixteen months ago almost to the day."

"Good thing you're not counting." Sarge walks backwards towards the gym door. "Time to knock the rust off. It's Fall Ball baby. Proving grounds."

"Hey Sarge?" He stops just short of the door. "Why do you call the weights 'girlfriends'?"

"Ha! Simple. They're like women. They have the power to break you down or build you up. But you found that out the hard way today, didn't you?"

8:06 A.M.

Tim and I pull into the apartment five parking spot.

"Shake, shower, snooze," Tim says, as we ascend the stairs amidst our neighbor's TV blaring Spanish commercials through open windows.

Tim was looking for a roommate just as I was ready to leave Mom's house to do my own thing. Perfect timing, but I wouldn't call us a perfect match. I do envy him at times, if I'm honest. A new girl seemingly every month. He can drink anyone under the table and be up for morning workouts like he got eight restful hours of sleep. I don't know how he does it or how his conscience lets him live with himself, but like I said, a small part of me envies him. I know that stuff won't get me to the bigs, though.

He unlocks the front door to our living room where a glass coffee table sits between the TV and a weathered black leather couch. The kitchen, not much to brag about either, is a six-by-six box comfortable enough for one guy to heat up leftover pizza while listening to low riders cruise down the street belching mariachi music.

Our bedrooms are buffered by a bathroom that keeps the late-night noises from Tim's room tolerable. That's when I welcome the neighbor's obnoxious Spanish TV blaring through my window. A song from my old church starts out, "This world is not my home, I'm just a passin' through . . ." I keep telling myself this place is something like that.

I make Tim and myself a couple of protein shakes and set his on a coaster in the living room. He opens a little baggy, packs a joint, and lights it up.

Really? At eight in the morning?

Through a thick cloud of smoke wreaking of dead skunk, Tim points to the living room flat screen TV where MLB 2K19 is loading. "You think you'll be in this video game someday?"

"I do. What about you?"

"Me? Yeah right. Must be nice knowing your future's set."

I army crawl my way over to the balcony sliding door and open it all the way. "I still have a lot to prove."

"Sorry." He swats away the smoke as if to purify the air. "How fast did you say you used to throw?"

"I touched 94 a few times but mostly sat 92-93."

"In high school? That's crazy. At least I'll be able to say I faced a future big leaguer."

I don't respond right away. That's what Sarge was talking about. Every guy will be measuring himself against me, trying to prove he belongs in the pros, too. "I'm only hitting 87 right now," I tell him. "Hopefully by spring I'll be back up in the 90s."

He toggles through the teams on screen. "Well, if you're as good as everyone says you are, we'll have no problem repeating at State."

"That's if Sarge doesn't kill me first."

We laugh.

The choo-choo train in my pocket rings out. A text from Mom. *You got a letter from Mack about a week ago. Just remembered. Sorry.*

I haven't heard from Mack in months nor have I reached out to him. I grab my smoothie. "I'll be back. Gotta run by my mom's house."

Traces of smoke exit his mouth as he picks up the second controller. "You don't want to play?"

"Not 'til I can play as me."

Mom's house is only fifteen minutes away, but far enough to give me the escape I need. On this particular drive, though, the distance plays against me, affording me time to overthink my long-awaited return to the mound tomorrow. Thanks to my time working one-on-one with Mack on my mental game, I know better than to let negative thoughts beat me. The rest of my drive I recall a few of the mental game nuggets he ingrained in me over the past year and a half . . .

At the highest level, the game's played less from the neck down and more from the neck up. The mound can be a lonely island, a place where a pitcher has only the ball and his thoughts for weapons. Hitters show no mercy. They don't care if you aren't feeling it that day. The baseball doesn't care either—it has no heartbeat.

You don't have to have your A-game. You'll rarely have everything working. The key is not to show it. It's about knowing what you have that night, whether it's your A, B, or C game, and dancing with her under the lights like it's prom night.

I exit the freeway to Mom's house. More of Mack's words swirl . . .

There's a difference between throwing and pitching. Throwing is like an aimless prayer while pitching is more like being a masterful painter. An artist. A con-artist. Methodical. Deceptive. Always toying with the hitter, presenting everything as a pleasurable fastball before changing speeds, trajectory, and location, keeping hitters off balance and tempting them to get themselves out. Pressure and pleasure.

Mack never missed an opportunity to mix in a Bible lesson when he could. *That's the same game plan the Devil uses in the world, too, pressuring and pleasuring us into striking ourselves out in life.* That one, for some reason, has always stuck with me.

There's an old ESPN Classic interview Mack has shown me a half-dozen times of Greg Maddux, a Hall of Fame Pitcher who threw under 90 mph for much of his career yet was one of the most menacing pitchers throughout the '90s. In the interview, Maddux discusses how at the beginning of his career it was hard for him to stay positive on the mound and think the right thoughts for the situation. But in the latter part of his career, he had so trained his mind that it was hard for him to think wrong thoughts. It just wasn't in him anymore. He pointed to his mental game as his greatest key to success.

That's a Hall of Fame mindset for you, Mack would tell me. He always glossed over the fact that it took Maddux fifteen years of learning from mistakes before he approached mental perfection. He accomplished mental mastery near the end of his career when his physical abilities were diminishing. I plan to master my mental game before hitting my prime.

I pull into Mom's neighborhood. The Southern California sun has been relentless this year. Yet, Mom's lawn, along with the entire neighborhood's, looks lush. Pristine. SoCal. I unlock the front door.

"Mom?" My echo returns uninterrupted off the vaulted ceilings. Only thin beams of light slip through the drapes leading to the backyard.

Since when does she shut the blinds?

I open them to the backyard that played out so much of my childhood. My lava pit. The Moon. And later, a whiffle ball field that magically turned into Angel Stadium. Dad taught me to love baseball back there. It's where our bond strengthened with each round of batting practice. Now, it's just an abandoned backyard.

My flip flops clap across the cherry wood toward the kitchen. The living room sofa pillows, the dining room table, and coffee tables are all in their proper places, yet everything seems out of place. In the kitchen, a single photo of me and Mom hangs on the fridge from high school graduation last year. A lifetime ago. Mack's letter lies atop a heap of bills and a bundle of mail with a sticky note: *Please get this mail to your father and remind him to change his address. Love you. Dinner tonight?*

I scribble a note that I'll be back for dinner, grab Dad's mail, then search the fridge. A quarter-bottle of white wine and not much else. I glance at the photo once more and lock the door behind me. My car is already sweltering when I return. With the air-conditioning on full blast, I tear the ends of Mack's envelope.

In Loving Memory
Suzanne Elizabeth Mack
1945-2019
PLEASE JOIN US IN CELEBRATING SUZIE'S LIFE,
SATURDAY, THE FOURTEENTH OF SEPTEMBER,
TWO THOUSAND AND NINETEEN
AT
11 O'CLOCK IN THE MORNING
The Crossing Church
2115 Newport Blvd, Costa Mesa, CA 92627
- Marcus Mack

The words shake in my hand as I reread them. I search the date again. Saturday, September 14, 2019. *Tomorrow?* I shift into drive and cue Siri to phone Coach Hill. He picks up on the third ring.

"Hey, Coach. It's Jacoby."

"Jacoby, what can I do for you?"

"I just found out my mentor's wife passed away."

"I'm sorry to hear that."

"Thank you. I know I'm supposed to pitch tomorrow, but the funeral's tomorrow and I feel like I need to be there to support him."

"Hey, I get it. Baseball can wait. We'll see you Monday. My condolences go out to your mentor."

"Thank you, Coach." *That went better than I thought.*

After my injury at the end of high school, the draft passed me up and the D-1 coach I'd committed to took a job in professional baseball, which forced me to forfeit my scholarship and settle for a local junior college, taking classes while my elbow recovered. My only criteria for school was that it be in Southern California where scouts could witness my comeback.

When Coach Hill's relentless recruiting calls came boasting of historic CCCAA State Championship runs, including last season's, and a track record of getting guys to pro ball, I signed after one visit to Orange Coast.

7:14 P.M.

The sun is slipping beneath the horizon when I return to the apartment after dropping off Dad's mail and hanging out with a buddy. Tim's heavy metal music rattles the front door when I reach the top step. I fight through the noise to the balcony, shutting the slider behind me. On my phone, the Angels are playing the Mariners. Should be an easy win. A few minutes later, through the lattice fencing, a female figure reaches the top stair and knocks on the front door.

"Tim won't be able to hear you. Hold up a sec." I open the door to the pair of soft blue eyes that rescued me during this morning's workout. She's better than Beyoncé. Everything in me screams to explore further, but I resist. "Fallon, right?"

She seems surprised I remember her name. "Is it Jake? From stats class?"

"Close. It's Jacoby."

She invites herself in, brushing against my shoulder, beer bottles clanking at her side. "Tim tells me you're good at baseball."

"He's never seen me play."

"Take it as a compliment. He rarely says anything nice about anyone."

"I will, then. What you got there?"

"Just a little pregame." She holds the bottles chest high. "Want one?"

"I'm good, thanks. Cold as the Rockies, right?" *Why would you say that?*

She purses her lips like she just bit into a lemon, "Something like that."

"Tim says nice things about you, too."

"Liar." Her lingering gaze almost seems to thank me for my lie. "You should sit by me in class next week, Jake."

"It's Jacoby."

She winks before heading to Tim's room. "I know."

My eyes stick around longer than they should. *Good for you, Tim. Good for you.* The music mutes momentarily as the crisp crack of bottle tops and clanking glass kicks off laughter before Tim's concert continues. Sounds fun. Harmless even. Maybe someday on my San Diego beachfront.

I return to my Angels game on the balcony, occasionally scrolling through Instagram on commercial breaks, out of habit more than anything. I find Fallon's profile and linger on her photos until I feel like a creeper, then switch back to the Angels game.

About fifteen minutes later, the sliding door flings open and Tim's music, followed by Fallon's laughter, spill onto the balcony. "You're coming out with us tonight," she shouts, hair not as neat as before.

Tim yells through the tunes, "Jacoby doesn't party."

She's puzzled. "But it's Friday night. Everyone's partying."

"Thanks for the offer. You guys have fun, though."

She leans over the balcony railing looking out towards the sunset. Her jean shorts squeeze her thighs.

Bounce your eyes away.

"Who's playing?" she asks, for sure catching my stare.

"Angels are losing."

"See, there's a reason to party."

"I'm an Angels fan."

"Well, then, there you go! Drinking's the best cure for when you're down."

So that's why you hang out with Tim. "I love your enthusiasm, but really, I'm good."

Tim pokes his head outside the slider. "Let's go. He'll come out for the Halloween beer pong tournament next month, right?"

"Sure, I'll come watch."

Fallon shakes her head at me. "Your loss." She follows Tim inside to down the rest of their beers. I drink her in one last time. When they leave, Fallon's fragrance remains. I shouldn't, but I allow my mind to replay her jean shorts up against the railing.

8:08 P.M.

When I arrive at Mom's house after night fall, the opening melody to *Jeopardy!* whines through the flat screen. "Smells like something's burning, Mom."

"The bread!" She searches frantically for a mitt. Burnt garlic clouds the kitchen. She slams the oven mitt down and puts her hand to her head. Eyes closed. Then, she slaps on an enthusiastic red lipstick smile. "Pasta with white sauce and salad will have to do."

"Still be better than the frozen pizza I was about to burn at my place," I grin, stepping forward to hug her until she's calm.

"Honey, let's eat in the living room tonight," she says, leaving my embrace to grab some silverware.

"Since when do you eat in there?"

"*Jeopardy!* is on, and I'm kind of on a hot streak."

"You got the hots for Alex Trebek?"

"Oh, shush. I'm talking about the game."

"I'm sure you can do better on Match.com."

"Watch it, young man."

The *Jeopardy!* categories flash across the screen, and we make a competition of it. She's impressive with her knowledge of random facts and time periods, but it all seems like a shallow victory. She speaks to the TV but never receives a personal response. A momentary satisfaction perhaps with a correct answer, but it's all gone in 30 minutes, not to return until Monday. She mutes the commercials and I break the silence.

"I'm going to a funeral tomorrow."

She looks up, mouth full of pasta. "Whose?"

"Mack's wife."

"Oh, honey." She wipes her mouth with a napkin. "I'm sorry to hear that. Have you talked to him?"

"I thought about texting him but didn't really know what to say. I'll talk to him after the funeral, I'm sure."

The show returns and she unmutes the TV. "Hold that thought, honey, I want to hear the new categories."

Really? *Because Jeopardy!'s more important than us actually talking*? At the next commercial break she mutes the TV again and twirls her noodles. "Okay, what were you saying honey? How's Mack?"

"I haven't talked to him yet."

"Oh, right. Gosh, I'm sure he's crushed."

"Hey, Mom . . ."

"Yeah, hon?"

I pause. *Just say it.* "What happened with you and dad?"

She twirls once more, takes a bite, chews slowly. Swallows. "I told you. You need to ask your father."

"At least give me your side of the story." My voice rises a bit.

"You're not the only one who's hurt you know."

She gets up and clears our plates without a word. I follow her to the kitchen. "You want me to come over and just watch TV?"

"Isn't hanging out enough?" She washes dishes furiously. "I just want to be with my boy."

"And watch a game show? We're not even talking. I don't like coming over here, Mom. It reminds me of everything I want to forget."

The side of her face turns rosy red as a tear drops to the dishes below. The faucet stops. She stares at the suds. "A relationship . . . a marriage . . . it takes two people. Two people who love each other very much. I'm not going to speak ill of your father. I'm not perfect myself. But if you want to know the truth—the honest truth—you need to ask him."

She turns on the faucet and continues washing dishes without so much as looking in my direction. I wrap my arms around her, kiss the back of her head, and go upstairs to retrieve my suit for the funeral.

Close to midnight, my head hits the pillow with two thoughts that won't let me fall asleep. My unanswered question about Mom and Dad, and, the fantasy of Fallon's smooth mocha skin stumbling into my sheets to help me forget everything.

Chapter 02

I FIDDLE WITH MY TIE near the back of the mega-church, nodding at the black suits and curvy dresses filling in the seats around me.

Older faces, friends of Mack and Suzanne most likely, take their time trekking down the center aisle toward the front of the stage, where floor-to-ceiling windows illuminate the podium. Above the podium, three screens hang from the rafters displaying a portrait of a middle-age woman with short blondish-white hair, hazel eyes, and a bright red blouse with matching lipstick and the caption "**Suzanne Mack 1945-2019**" underneath.

Mack is in the front row, sitting between a woman much older than him and a girl, maybe my age, with straight long blonde hair. Whispers bounce off the walls as the stage lighting dims and a woman solemnly makes her way to the piano for the opening hymn. Those in the first few rows stand on cue. We follow in the back. After several worship songs, the pastor invites us to take our seats and over the next 30 minutes, several of Suzanne's friends and family celebrate her life with personal stories revealing the type of woman Mack shared his life with.

Finally, Mack climbs the steps to the podium and faces us. He's aged since I last saw him. His typically tan cheeks are rosy. Eyes wet. Human. He adjusts the microphone, sips from a miniature water bottle, and with a clearing of the throat, scans our dimly lit faces.

"I'll always remember Suzie's words right before she agreed to marry me," he begins. "She told me, in her Southern style—the kind of style that still sounds sweet even when you're being yelled at . . . "

A subdued laugh moves through the crowd.

"She told me, 'Now, before you go sliding that shiny ring on my finger, I want you to know one thing Marcus Bartholomew Mack—'"

He pauses. Smiles. "'I'll always love God more than I'll ever love you.'"

My lips curl up at the sides.

"Now in that moment, being second place to God or anyone else sort of rubbed my grapefruit-sized ego the wrong way, but I would've agreed to just about anything to get that ring on her finger and kiss her."

His bold blue eyes soften on the HD screens above him.

"I didn't fully understand her words at the time. But as she began to open my eyes to the Scriptures and demonstrate what it meant to walk with God on a moment-by-moment basis, her promise to me stood far more faithful than the one I vowed to her."

Mack pauses, looks at the podium, perhaps at some notes, then back at us.

"In Genesis 2:18, it was God who first recognized man's need for companionship. Not man. That's God for you. Always ahead of the need. And when He created Eve for Adam, He didn't just throw something together hoping it'd work. Genesis says God created Eve to be a 'help *meet*' for Adam. That phrase is an interesting one. *Help* means to aid, to support, to give strength to. And the word *meet* means adequate, rightly suited, or fit for the job. When God created woman, He created a support system perfectly suited to strengthen man. And, when God created Suzie, He spared no expense in making her perfectly suited to bring out the best in me. I can only hope I did the same for her.

"As many of you know, up until she got too sick, Suzie ran a weekly sports ministry on top of working her regular job. How she found time to do it all, I'll never fully grasp. She was truly industrious. Some of my favorite moments were sitting in the back like one of the athletes, listening to her teach. She never looked more beautiful than when she fed those kids God's Word. And of course, being a Southern woman, you *know* she fed their bellies, too."

A ripple of laughter sweeps through the church.

"Something I admired about Suzie was that, despite knowing all my faults, she never held them over my head or bad-mouthed me to her friends. Why not? Only one way. She loved God more than she ever loved me and knew that *Proverbs 17* says that those who seek love cover up offenses but those who repeat a matter separate close friends. We were best of friends."

He holds a teary smile.

"I could share anything with Suzie. Some listen to talk, while others listen to listen. She was the best listener. Even to things she didn't want to hear. Difficult things, but things we needed to hash out before bed. She never liked letting something fester even if it seemed easier to sweep under the rug. She made sure we fell asleep each night looking into each other's eyes rather than at our nightstands."

He finishes his miniature water bottle, places it beneath the podium, and pulls out a new one.

"I look back now and understand how we were able to endure

the truly tough times, and how important it really was that she chose to love God more than me. Like when we lost our son."

His voice weakens. "When Sammy passed away, I buried myself in my work, thinking that if I could just be the best at what I do, it would fill the hole Sammy left. But that meant distancing myself from Suzie. And even worse, I distanced myself from God. I wanted to heal on my own. That was selfish of me. Stupid. Arrogant.

"How did she stay strong for both of us through it all? She loved God more than she loved me and knew God's Word says man will fail us but God never does. She showed me what God's grace is by loving me when I didn't deserve to be loved. It was her free gift to me that she'd freely received from God. She was able to comfort me with the same comfort she'd received from the Scriptures. She knew it wasn't her job to heal me. Only God could mend a shattered heart."

Muffled whimpers move through the aisles.

Don't blink. Don't blink. Too late. I wipe a tear.

"It wasn't until many selfish years later that I fully grasped what her words meant the day I proposed. You see, when a person loves God more than they love us, it's the kindest thing they can offer. Sometimes, in our egotistical minds we think we're supposed to be all things to all people. Their happiness, their bank, their counselor, and their comedian. News flash. We can't. But God can."

He pauses, gently holding a white handkerchief in his left hand.

"Our Heavenly Father can be all things to all people. Christianity is not a religion. It's a relationship. A way of a Father with His children. That's the relationship He desires with each one of us. When someone learns to love God more than they love us . . . they allow their words and actions to be governed by God's Word rather than controlled by emotions. It's not easy. But Suzie seemed to have it mastered. It's a mindset that lives on a higher plane, on higher ground.

"I guess what I'm trying to say is, when a spouse loves God more than they love us, it gives us the freedom to *not* have to be perfect. It certainly brought a greater enjoyment and appreciation to our marriage. Once I really grasped what she'd been so faithful to demonstrate year after year, month after month, day after day, moment by moment, it allowed me to be the best man I knew to be and to let God handle the heavy lifting. I'm so thankful to have learned that from Suzie. And, after many years of witnessing her gracious example, I too, have learned to love God more than any one person. That's what will get me through this dark time." His eyes close. "I am so thankful to you for teaching me that, honey."

Mack retrieves his Bible from under the podium. "I've blabbered on far too long already. Bear with me a few more moments as we round third. When Sammy passed away, Suzie read me 1 Thessalonians 4:13-18 almost every day for a long time. I'll share it with you now in hopes that it will offer you the same encouragement it brings me now."

The passage in the NIV appears on screen.

> *Brothers and sisters, we do not want you to be uninformed about those who sleep in death, so that you do not grieve like the rest of mankind, who have no hope. For we believe that Jesus died and rose again, and so we believe that God will bring with Jesus those who have fallen asleep in him. According to the Lord's word, we tell you that we who are still alive, who are left until the coming of the Lord, will certainly not precede those who have fallen asleep. For the Lord himself will come down from heaven, with a loud command, with the voice of the archangel and with the trumpet call of God, and the dead in Christ will rise first. After that, we who are still alive and are left will be caught up together with them in the clouds to meet the Lord in the air. And so we will be with the Lord forever. Therefore encourage one another with these words.*

Mack closes his Bible, still admiring the cover like a family photo.

"Family . . . friends . . . when Suzie used to read those words to me—God's Words—they encouraged me to look forward to Christ's return as an ever-present reality rather than some distant event. Every morning Suzie would take my face between her warm hands"—his arms outstretch as if gently holding a small basketball—"and look me in the eyes with that big Southern smile, and remind me, 'It could be today, Marcus! Christ could come back today!'

"So, to all of you, remember, a lifetime is a string of moments. And at any moment—*any moment!*—Christ could come back for us. Whatever you're going through right now, be assured that you can endure for just one more moment because in the twinkling of an eye, Christ could return to gather His people and so shall we ever be with the Lord. What a hope we have. Sure and steadfast. It doesn't take the sting of death away. But it sure softens its blow."

He places his Bible under the podium. I breathe in deeply, feeling like I've just spent years getting to know Suzanne, someone who loved Mack and took care of his heart. Someone, I will never meet. Her hazel eyes return on screen. It's even harder to look now.

"I'm so grateful to each one of you for celebrating Suzie's life with me today." Mack says. "I'd like to welcome you to gather at my house for refreshments immediately following the service. The address is on the bulletin. God bless you."

On the walk back to my car, Sarge's words run through my head about those 45-pound plates: "They're similar to women. They have the ability to break you down or build you up."

Mack had found one that built him up.

SATURDAY AFTERNOON, 4 P.M.

I get some homework done for a couple hours at my favorite lunch spot before I head over to Mack's house for the reception. When I arrive, only a few cars remain. His house, a long single-story with a blinding white coat offset by a navy trim, seems a beam of light during a dark time.

I step through the front door to a few voices still gathered around a dining room table covered with snack foods and beverages. Loud colored walls of orange, blue, and red framed in white baseboards scream *Home and Garden* magazine. Suzanne's choices, I'd guess. Mack is in the middle of a sea of champagne flutes and tightly held tissues. He spots me and breaks away from conversation.

"Jacoby. Glad you could make it."

"Mack." We embrace. "It's good to see you. How you holding up?"

"I'm blessed, brother. Truly blessed."

He reaches for an ice water on the black marble island. "Thanks for coming."

"It's the least I could do. Sorry I'm a little late."

"I'm just glad you're here." He looks over his shoulder. "What do you say we catch up in my office for a bit?"

"I don't want to keep—"

He places his hand on my shoulder and leads me down a hallway lit by skylights. "Don't worry. I can use the break."

Near the end of the hall, he opens two doors from the middle—like a coat-tailed butler from a Disney movie. "After you."

More skylights illuminate the forest green carpet and cause countless trophies to sparkle. Signed baseballs and bats line mahogany shelves. Neatly pressed jerseys hang from the walls.

"Where'd you get all this?"

"Almost 40 years of memories. Some of the memorabilia are my own collection, but most are from appreciative clients. Suzie always liked seeing it all on display. I like to think it reminded her of why I did what I did, which gave me some leeway to be away so much. It's more for her than for me. I lived it."

Mack hangs back, allowing me to tour his mini-museum, mouth slightly ajar. A Rawlings glove is encased in glass and enshrined in gold. It's signed and has 'Strive for 5' written in black Sharpie below the signature.

Mack shoulders up to me. "One of my minor-league clients sent this to me after he retired. He never made it to the show. I met him when he was in Single-A, playing shortstop. He was homesick like crazy and surrounded by competition he'd never imagined. A cannon for an arm but couldn't catch a cold—something like 70 errors that season. That many errors will have you questioning more than your ability."

"So, he reached out to you?"

"Yep. We developed a better mental approach that he bought into, practiced, and mastered. A simple suggestion really."

I tap the glass. "Does it have to do with 'Strive for 5'?"

"It's a simple grading system to help him play the game within the game. Instead of wondering *if* he'd field the ball, the focus became just *how well* he'd field it on a scale of 1 to 5.

"It must've worked."

"After he got in the habit of challenging himself to strive for five with each groundball, the thought of not fielding it rarely crossed his mind. And when those thoughts of fear did come, he learned to kick them out and allow the fun back in."

"I like it."

"You can do it with your pitches, you know. The break, the drop, your release point, the movement, the deep breath. Just about anything. Keeps the focus on the right thing."

"I'll try it out. I was actually supposed to throw an inning this morning, but I wouldn't have missed this for anything."

"Then it means a lot to me that you're here." He wanders around the room, running a finger on the occasional memorabilia, perhaps checking for dust. "I look at all this stuff and see the faces that go with the names. Humble athletes eager to get the most out of their abilities. Ready to put in the work."

He looks back in my direction. "There's a difference between knowing and doing. Only the ones who truly want to grow ever get busy doing. But it separates them from the rest. The mental game isn't complicated. But it isn't easy, either. It doesn't live on paper. It comes to life in performance. In the doing."

I examine the Rawlings Gold Glove and ponder his words. The silence becomes too uncomfortable for me, hanging in the air between us like a high pop fly in the infield on sunny day with no one taking charge.

"My parents split up," I blurt out. "About three months ago. I haven't talked about it much. Not even with them. They don't talk about it at all."

Soon, Mack's hand rests on my shoulder. "Why don't we sit down for a few minutes."

"You've got guests . . . I don't know why I said anything. Today's about Suzanne."

"Suzie's not here anymore." He gestures for me to sit. "And, I've already spent time with everyone who's still here."

I glance back at the shimmering Gold Glove once more before settling in across from him. "I guess things had been bad for a while, but they kept it under wraps pretty much until the day they sat me down and told me my dad was moving out."

"They didn't say why?"

"Nothing. After Dad left, I asked my mom a couple times, but she kept telling me to ask him.'"

"How are you holding up?"

I smile and blink rapidly. A framed poem hangs from the wall behind Mack, but the words begin to swim. "Numb, most days. I don't know."

"Understandable." Mack breathes deeply, perhaps searching for what to say next. But there's nothing to be said. "Where are you living now?"

I wipe my eyes and clear my throat. "With a teammate. Pretty good shortstop."

"Good situation?"

"Better than home."

He says nothing at first. "I remember when I left home for the first time. Plenty of freedom but endless temptations."

"Yeah. Found that out real quick. None of that's for me though. I'm just focused on getting drafted next June."

"Drafted, huh?" He flashes perhaps his biggest smile of the day as he leans forward in his swivel chair.

I point to a vacancy high on his wall. "June 1st Mack, my jersey's going right there."

"I don't doubt it." His face turns from pure joy to contemplative. "Do you plan to speak with your father?"

"I could, but it's not gonna fix anything. Time heals all, right?"

"Not necessarily. Time can also allow bitterness and pain to fester. If you're going to fully focus on the draft . . . It might be worth it to get some answers so it's not eating you up inside. Unfortunately, this isn't the kind of situation that just goes away with time."

I wish it were.

Framed on the wall beside the poem is a sun-faded photo of an attractive couple smiling back at me. She's got big blonde curls, and he's sporting a dark mustache. From the way they're dressed, to the fuzziness of the photo, it's the epitome of the '80s. "Is that you and Suzanne?"

He swivels around. "July 27th, 1980. Old Yankee Stadium. That was my first ever client to make the bigs. Came up that day with Seattle."

"You remember the date?"

"You never forget a date like that. You won't either when it's your turn." He turns back to me. "Suzie didn't travel with me much, but she wouldn't have missed that one for the world. She was my biggest fan. And I was hers."

He reaches for a photo of her on his desk and admires it. "I'm sorry you two never got a chance to meet."

"She sounds incredible. Today you mentioned something about it being your faith that held you two together through the ups and downs. Where do you think my parents went wrong? They're Christians."

His eyes meet mine. "Unfortunately, I'm not qualified to speak on anyone's marriage but my own. Each one's different. And no one's is perfect. Mine definitely wasn't. But for us, it came down to two individuals loving God above all else."

"Yeah."

"When God's at the center, it's no longer about who's right but about what's right—according to God's standard, not our own. I can't tell you how many times Suzie and I had to put our egos aside and go to the Scriptures to see what God had to say rather than try to win every battle. When a couple has the humility to make the Scriptures the ultimate standard, it'll soften hearts and heal wounds."

He sets her photo back down, adjusting it until it's just right.

I walk to the window. "I think that's the nicest garden I've ever seen."

"Suzie was the green thumb. You should see it at night. That lattice over the deck lights up. We had some wonderful get-togethers back there. I've arranged for the gardener to take care of it while I'm gone."

I turn to Mack. "Wait, you're leaving?"

"Headed back east. I promised Suzie I'd care for her mother. She's not doing so well herself. Doctor says she's only got about six months."

"Was that the older lady sitting next to you at the church?"

"That's her. We're flying out tomorrow. I'll be there as long as it's beneficial."

"Can we still talk?"

"Of course. I'll be a phone call away."

We hug it out before he leads me back through the hallway toward the growing chatter. I make my way toward the front door.

"Jacoby . . ."

I turn back. He raises his water glass. "To new beginnings."

"To new beginnings."

03

MONDAY, SEPTEMBER 16, 2019, 2:31 P.M.

Wendell Pickens Field, Orange Coast College

CHAINSMOKERS RADIO BLARES THROUGHOUT the clubhouse. Dented lockers hosting musty baseball cleats, gloves, and far-away dreams of pro ball form a rectangle around two beat-up couches facing each other. The thwack of the bathroom stalls 10 feet away wafts the pleasant smell of piss my way, reminding me how far I am from the D-1 sanctuaries I'd visited in high school. Still, I'm closer now than I've ever been to the big leagues.

Here comes Coach Jenkins, our pitching coach, hobbling toward my locker with his cane, already making me smile without saying anything. If Jackie Robinson were still alive, they could be brothers.

"Out of all the dang music you getta choose from, you goin' with this, Jacky boy?"

At some point I'd become either Johnson, Jack, Jacky boy, or Bonus Baby to everyone on this team. Pretty much anything but my actual name—Jacoby (juh-Kobe).

Coach Jenkins smacks my calf on the way by. "You do what you gotta do to get your mind right though, cuz you gon' face some adversity today. They's already scouts in them stands waiting to see you throw. I ain't never seen that this early in Fall Ball."

"Thanks for the confidence boost, Jenksy."

"My pleasure, son. Always one pitch at a time. That's all we ever have time for."

He'd either invented the mental game in his younger days or picked it up along the way, but he resembled Mack with his little sayings. This year he was experimenting with letting the starting pitcher pick the pre-game clubhouse music. A sort of owning-your-performance-from-the-beginning experiment. I'm not so sure he's a fan of the Chainsmokers. All depends on how I pitch today, I guess.

When he hobbles off, I turn back to my mental preparation routine I'd once penned in Mack's office. He might be on the East Coast by now, but as far as I know, he's right in my ear.

When you're putting on your cleats . . . put on your cleats. When you're putting on your hat . . . put on your hat. Be where you're at, Jacoby. In the now. Be where you're at.

In my locker, *1PW* is written on my dry erase board. An acronym meaning one pitch warrior from one of my favorite mental game authors, Justin Dehmer. It reminds me of my mission to stay in the present moment for one quality pitch at a time. If I can manage that, the rest should take care of itself.

The clubhouse is full of nervous chatter when news spreads about the pro scouts sitting in the stands. The pigeons crapping in my stomach seem to believe it's Game 7 of the World Series. Not because of the scouts. I'm used to them by now. It's more due to not having thrown to a live batter in a year and a half.

I double-knot my cleats as Mack's voice cautions: *Either make them all big games or all just games. Either way, treat them all the same. The baseball doesn't care. Neither should you.* At least the pigeons inside me are relieved to hear that. Or just relieved.

I grab my glove and head for the field. My spikes sink into the artificial turf that's burning through my cleats from the final days of summer heat. *Today's your day, Jacoby. Your moment. Let's do it.*

"Ten till go time," Coach Hill shouts. "Get hot."

The outfield plays host to stretching bodies in orange practice shirts, white pants cuffed at the knees, and navy blue stockings. More of Mack's messages flood in: *It doesn't matter how you feel. Give me 100 percent of what you have today. You don't have to be great. Good pitches will get the job done. Make the ball your weapon. When it comes to pitching, there are no nice guys. Attack. Attack. Attack.*

His volume is turned up even louder once I hit the bullpen for warmup tosses with my catcher Shawn Bauer. After about 30 pitches, a mix of fastballs and changeups, I signal to Bauer that I'm good. All I can do is be comforted by this Mackism: *Bullpen accuracy isn't necessarily an indicator of what'll happen on the game mound.* I take a deep cleansing breath before jogging to the mound. Sure enough, at least 10 scouts are gathered behind home plate with radar guns in hand, ready to lift with my first warmup pitch.

Coach Jenkins flips me a freshly mudded baseball and slowly canes his way to his position behind me to call balls and strikes. "You got twenty bullets to work with today. We're easing that elbow of yours back in. All fastballs and changeups. Mix up ya speeds. Move it around and compete."

I dig out a small niche for footing in front of the pitching rubber before beginning my warmup tosses. There was a time after surgery when a baseball felt like a foreign object. But the familiar feel has returned, like picking up conversation with an old friend. Today, the ball comes out smooth and effortlessly.

Mack's voice chimes in: *Nervousness and excitement feel the same. Choose to feel excited. Use it to your advantage.*

On my last warmup pitch, Bauer throws a bullet down to second. I take off my sweat-drenched cap to wipe my forehead under the relentless sun and steal a peek at the scouts who are discussing their radar gun readings.

You're ready, Jacoby. Day one, pitch one, on the road to The Show. You and me God.

A slender sophomore digs into the left-handed batter's box. Bauer flashes a thumb and moves to the outside corner. Fastball away. *Breathe. See your target. Release out front.*

"Steerike!" Coach Jenkins calls from behind me.

The ball thuds back into my Wilson A2000 webbing. *Stay right there. One pitch at a time. Breathe.*

Again, thumb. Fastball away.

"Ball!"

My throwing hand retracts to my release point. I freeze it right there with pointer and middle fingers forked. *Release out there.*

The next pitch, a fastball intended to be low and away runs inside, missing badly, followed by a pitch fouled straight back. *He's right on it. Mix up your speeds.* I step off and turn around toward the outfield scoreboard flashing all zeros except for the 2-2 count. I toe the rubber, again. Pinky, up in the zone. Fastball up and in. *Sure about that?*

The doubt doesn't leave as I wind up and deliver. *Bam!* The ball meets the batter's hard plastic helmet, silencing everyone as he goes down. Acid spills into my gut, bringing me to a knee. The coaching staff jogs over to check the batter for signs of concussion. After a minute, he gets up and jogs to first. *He's fine. Get back up there and throw.*

But my muscles aren't listening. They're busy strangling the ball without my permission. *Two strikes and you do that? Can't happen.*

Next to dig in is a right-handed batter. Bauer signals for a fastball away. I come set. Still no feel for the laces on the ball. Check the runner. Check the plate. Runner. Plate. *How could you miss your spot that badly? Don't hit this guy, too.* I throw the next pitch straight down Broadway.

"Runner!" the infield shouts in unison. *Ping!* The ball is scalded through the vacated right side of the infield, a hit-and-run executed to perfection.

"Quit being a spectator and back up third, Johnson," Coach Hill barks from the dugout.

By the time I get there, the runner from first is already dusting off his pant leg on third. Now, there's runners on the corners. *Am I even gonna get an out?* The ball thuds back in my glove from the third baseman, and I pace toward the mound where Coach Jenkins is already waiting for me with gold-plated dentures. "Welcome back, Jacky boy!"

"Funny." I slam the ball in my glove as sweat drips from my bill.

"What you so darn worried about, son? No one's scored yet."

"I had two strikes on that guy when I hit him."

"That was two batters ago. You still try'na get him out?"

My cleat manicures the mound as he talks.

"You done walked back to this mound like a chicken try'na cut off his own head. These guys'll sniff that out and jump on ya. Can't be showing them scouts that, either. What's your job, anyhow?"

"To get outs."

"No it ain't. Your job's to prevent runs—not baserunners." Coach Jenkins checks his pitch count clicker. "What you gonna do with them fourteen bullets you got left? You goin' try to strike out the past or pitch right here, right now?"

His words fade as Mack's warnings about the deceptive ease of the mental game haunt my mind. *It's easy to write 'Remember to breathe' on paper in the comfort of my office. But when everything's falling apart out there, you'll find out how hard it is to slow down and get back to the present moment.*

Once again, Mack's right. It's war out here.

Coach Jenkins speaks up again. "Let's see what you made of right now. Good chance that runner on third gonna score, but who cares? Besides, your team ain't even hit yet."

His golden grill cools me off. My hands now hold the baseball like an egg, smoothing and rotating the laces slowly.

Damage control, Jacoby. One pitch at a time. Love the moment. Nowhere else you'd rather be than right here.

The next batter, a lefty already committed to a D-1 school next year, loves hunting fastballs early in the count. Bauer signals for a fastball up and in. Mack's voice coaches me, *Sometimes, throwing softer is the most aggressive move.*

I shake off Bauer, wanting to go soft away. I come to the set position, peek at the runner at first, then at the runner dancing off third base. Mack's voice is running through my head: *Everything happens twice. First in your mind. Then in real life. Control how you see it in your mind. Then make it happen for real.*

The moment slows even more. Home plate looks close enough to reach out and place the ball where I want. The catcher's mitt, a Rawlings rawhide, begs for the baseball like a hungry mouth at dinner. In my mind's eye, the ball starts down the middle and breaks low and away with a blue flame trailing it.

I release the ball with aggressive arm action and a loose grip. *Pang!* A weak pop up down the left field line. I jog backwards to back up home plate. Fair or foul? Fair or foul? Slow motion turned all the way up. My left fielder sprints in to make a spectacular diving grab just outside the foul line. The runner on third is heads up and tags to score, 1-0. The ball settles back into my glove. Man on first, one away. Thirteen pitches left. I take to the mound like victory is already mine, giving Coach Jenkins a wink of confidence. He winks back and nods.

I run the next batter, another lefty, to a 1-2 count. Shawn signals for a fastball up. I come set. Check the runner. Deliver.

"Runner!" the infield shouts.

The batter swings and misses, strike three. Then Bauer zings a seed past my ear to the second base bag, where Tim is there to meet the ball with a perfect tag to nail the runner by a foot.

"Atta baby!" I shout, heading toward the dugout on a jog. A strike 'em-out, throw-'em out double-play. One run on 11 pitches.

"Good job," Coach Hill says, as I receive high fives in the dugout. "That's it for the day."

After the intra-squad is over, Coach Jenkins lets me know there's someone wanting a word with me outside the clubhouse. I recognize Branch Calderone, a big-time scout and national cross-checker for the Angels. He first introduced himself to me in my freshman year in high school after one of my best outings on varsity.

"You looked good out there today," he says, shaking my hand. "Not quite shades of the past, but it'll come."

"Thanks for coming out, Mr. Calderone."

"After all these years you're still calling me that? Branch is fine."

"When you draft me next year I'll call you Branch. How 'bout that?"

He chuckles. "I see your confidence didn't need physical therapy. How's the elbow?"

"It's good. I'm on a pitch count right now, and they're not letting me throw any breaking stuff yet."

"Good. No use rushing it. I just wanted to stop by and let you know we have our eyes on you. We'd love nothing more than a hometown boy pitching for the Angels."

Now that was cool to hear.

6:39 P.M.
Northbound on the 405 Freeway

On my drive to the apartment, I replay my outing. Most pitchers would chalk it up as one run scored on 11 pitches, call it a day, and hit the video games. But I'm not like most pitchers. Mack won't let me be. He taught me that every outing has its good and bad moments and to not squeeze every ounce of knowledge from them would be a waste of good information. He warned me, though, that evaluating a performance, especially the ones you're not proud of, are about as enjoyable as hearing your own voice on playback.

"Call Mack," I command Siri, as I trudge along the jammed freeway during rush hour. A few rings later, a muffled voice sounds through the speakers.

"Jacoby, good evening."

I totally forgot he's back East. "Sorry, Mack. I can call back tom—."

"It's fine. My body's not on East Coast time yet. How are you?"

"Stuck in traffic. But I threw my first inning today."

"How'd it go?"

"A little different from how we drew it up, but for the first day back, I'll take it."

A softened I-told-you-so laughs through the speakers. "Good to hear. What were you happy with?"

"I thought I bounced back well from adversity."

"How so?"

I recall for Mack the highs and lows of my 11-pitch inning.

"What moment are you most proud of?" he asks.

"What *moment*?" My eyes run from side mirror to side mirror, checking the car headlights around me. "I had first and third, no outs. I told myself there was no one else I'd rather have out there than me. I believed it. Really believed it. Kind of gave me a confidence boost and helped me slow things down."

"It's nice when your mind is your ally, isn't it?"

"For sure. Just gotta keep working it."

"That's right. Hey, I picked up a pretty good book at the airport on my way here. It's not a baseball book but it talked about learning to focus on one thing. It got me thinking—"

"That's always trouble."

"True. But hear me out. It got me thinking how you might simplify pitching. From today, what one thing, if done consistently, would've made everything about pitching easier?"

I flick on the blinker to merge over to a faster-moving lane, but the gap closes quickly. SoCal drivers see blinkers like sharks smell blood and speed up to not let you in. "I can think of 30."

"Choose one."

Several things come to mind. *Better location of my fastball on the first pitch? Not caring about runners? Not beaning batters with two strikes? Forgetting about the scouts?* "I guess my goal today was to throw one quality pitch at a time. It actually worked well when things were going good."

"And when they weren't?"

"I forgot my game plan and stopped breathing. Dwelled on the guy I beaned. Worried what the scouts in the stands were talking about. Sped up between pitches. Missed spots. Listened to that negative voice chirping at me."

"Ah yes, that evil voice strikes again. I think you're on to something with the one-quality-pitch-at-a-time thing, though. Sounds like you know what to do. It just needs refining and practice."

"Yeah. When I was playing in the present, it was definitely easier to let go of what just happened and move on to the next pitch. I was focused on telling myself what to do. I kept things simple."

"What you just described is you playing at your best, or what I call playing in 'the green'—as in green lights. The other stuff—the hit batter, speeding up, all that—are yellow and red lights. What did your negative voice tell you when things started going bad?"

My right foot eases on and off the brake pedal at 5 mph as I recall hitting that batter. "My catcher called for a 2-2 fastball up-and-in. Right before I threw the pitch, I said, 'I don't know about this.'"

"What tense does that statement suggest?"

"Future?"

"Correct. The ball hadn't even left your hand yet, and you were already predicting a bad outcome."

"Yeah, you're right."

"Doubt is definitely a yellow light mentality. Did you doubt any of the previous pitches?"

"No. I was just throwing."

"That's you at your best. When you're just throwing. A pitcher's job isn't to think. It's to pitch. That's why he's called a pitcher. Not a thinker."

The East Coast's made Mack a little spicy. I like it.

Mack continues, "It's important that you build an awareness for what takes you out of green and puts you in yellow or red. Bad calls, cheap hits over the infield, missing your spots, errors behind you—all those tend to be yellows. Red lights tend to be any of these happening on consecutive plays. In other words, red lights are basically amplified yellows that go unnoticed, like speeding down the freeway at 80 jamming out to a good song. And, before you know it, you've got the cops behind you."

"Wait . . . so, how can I be aware of something I'm not aware of?"

"It comes down to your between-pitch routines. Your routines remind you to check in with yourself every pitch, release what just happened, breathe, and refocus on what's important now. It might take focusing on a little pebble in the dirt until you're ready to throw again. A few words of self-encouragement tend to help. You're not always going to feel like being nice to yourself but the great ones aren't concerned with feelings. They can feel later. In the moment, you have to tell yourself what to do, regardless of how you feel. Actually a firm kick in the butt can be pretty effective, too. Like when a mom uses your—"

"Middle name. We've talked about this before."

"On more than one occasion, I'm sure. Well, listen, this old man needs to get to bed. Your homework's to write out a list of your green, yellow, and red lights. Write down when you get them, how they impact your body language, your focus, and what you say to yourself. Then, I want you to build a simple routine that will allow you to recognize when you're not in a green-light situation, when you need to release your yellows or reds, and how you can refocus back in green for the next pitch. Recognize, release, refocus. Just remember the three R's of routines. This stuff doesn't just go for baseball. Practice it in all areas of your life."

"Thanks Mack. I will." I go to hang up, but he keeps talking.

"Remember, quality pitches start with quality thoughts, and you're only ever one thought away from being at your best. Got it?"

"Got it."

"Go get some God's Word in you, too. Let's talk next week."

"Sounds good."

"One more thing. Are you going to that campus ministry?"

"I got the email today about the first meeting, but I haven't looked at it yet."

"Don't let it slide. Alright then, get some rest. Congrats on your first day back."

"Thanks. Hey Mack—"

Click.

Dang. I never got to ask how he's been doing since the memorial service. While keeping my eyes open on the road, I start praying:

Heavenly Father, I lift up Mack. I pray for his heart, that you would mend it and give him the strength to care for Suzanne's mom. I pray he gets the rest he needs. In Christ's name, amen.

7:26 P.M.
Back at My Apartment

From my phone, I open the email from campus sports ministry. "Please join us this Sunday, September 22 at 7 p.m., where we'll *Go 2 God* together and make Him a priority amidst the busyness of life and sport. Looking forward to seeing everyone! Much love in Christ, Everly."

Last spring, on Mack's recommendation, I had joined a sports ministry called *Go 2 God*, which we call G2G for short. I kept going, I'll admit, for a reason that wasn't entirely related to studying the Bible.

Everly Stevens, the sophomore libero on the volleyball team, was that reason.

A few of us from the baseball team went last week to the home volleyball game where Everly was an absolute beast on the court— constantly sacrificing her body diving for loose balls. In the few brief conversations we've had, I've learned two things about her: She loves God and she loves sports.

And, she doesn't suck to look at in volleyball spandex, either.

Chapter 04

SUNDAY, SEPTEMBER 22, 7 P.M.

G2G Meeting on Campus

BIBLE IN HAND, I mingle with a few athletes before spotting Everly lighting up the other side of the room in conversation. Her wavy hair is tossed up in a thick dirty blonde ponytail still wet from the shower. We lock eyes. She beams a smile, waves, and seems to look for a reason to break off conversation.

"I was wondering if you'd be here tonight," she says, giving me a friendly hug.

"I made it. Good game the other night."

She smirks and rolls her eyes. "It's early. We're still finding our groove."

"You got some good bruises at least."

"Yeah, my boyfriend can get rough with me sometimes." Her eyes wait for my response. "Totally kidding. The gym floor's a little harder than that soft turf you boys play on. How's your elbow? It was your elbow, right?"

"Good memory. Yeah, all cleared. It's felt good so far."

She glances at her watch, then behind me. "Are you sitting with anyone?"

"Nope."

"Then sit next to me."

We take seats among a dozen chairs forming a circle and catch up a bit more. Nothing special. She peeks at her watch again. Then, she stands and shouts, "Alright, everyone. Let's get started."

My eyes widen as I recall her name being at the end of the email. I'm sitting next to the new leader of *G2G* and the center of attention. On the mound, it never bothers me to be on center stage, but for some reason it's not quite the same when it comes to Bible stuff. Following Everly's opening prayer, we go around the circle introducing ourselves, saying where we're from, our sport, and one way we feel God is currently working in our lives. I don't have much to say about that last part, though.

Everly is clearly in her element. "Thank you all for sharing, and thank you for investing your Sunday night to get into God's Word together. I know it might not be the most convenient night of the week, but let's be honest, it's always a battle to make time for God."

I angle my chair so I don't have to crane my neck to listen to her.

"It's been a crazy semester for me already personally, but I finally got it together and am so excited to be with you all," she continues. "Can you believe it's almost October?"

Nods circle the chairs.

"Unfortunately, this year we only get this room for two hours a month, so we're going to meet every other week instead of every week like last year. But that doesn't mean we can't form small groups to meet at coffee shops. If anything, it'll push us to be more accountable to each other. I had the summer to spend in prayer with my mentor knowing I'd be taking on this role, and I've settled on the theme verse for this year. If you have your Bibles, let's turn to Romans 12:2."

Pages flip as she waits for everyone to get there. "Okay, I'll read it out of the New International Version: 'Do not conform to the pattern of this world, but be transformed by the renewing of your mind. Then you will be able to test and approve what God's will is—his good, pleasing and perfect will.'

"There's a ton to this verse and really to the entire chapter. Let's take a few minutes to read Chapter 12 silently to ourselves to get a feel for where this verse sits and then we can discuss it as a group, okay?"

For the next five minutes, it's a library apart from the air-conditioner clicking on. In the silence, I realize that it's only the second or third time I've opened my Bible since moving out of Mom's house. I don't know why I haven't been doing it more often. Mack always tells me, *"If you're too busy for God, you're too busy to be living."*

Everly breaks the silence. "What do you guys think?"

Shy smiles circle the room. Finally, a softball player chimes in. "I like how our theme verse comes after the first verse that says, 'Therefore, I urge you, brothers and sisters, in view of God's mercy, to offer your bodies as a living sacrifice, holy and pleasing to God—this is your true and proper worship.'"

"Me too," Everly agrees. "What stuck out about it to you, Rebecca?"

"I like how God is asking us to be living sacrifices for Him. Jesus sacrificed His life for us. The least we could do is live for Him."

"That's really cool. So true. How might verse one help us better understand verse two, anyone?"

I busy myself in my Bible, peeking up to see others doing the same. Someone else, a cross country runner I'd guess from his slight build, raises a bony hand.

Everly points. "Go ahead, Connor."

"It almost seems like verse one and two build off each other. Like, if we're going to give ourselves as living sacrifices, we can't conform to the ways of the world."

"Good point," Everly says. "Did anyone catch where it says to give your *bodies* as a living and holy sacrifice? It's in the plural, but it's speaking to individuals."

"I saw that too," Connor says.

I bet you did Connor.

Everly searches her notes. "My mentor shared with me that it's a figure of speech emphasizing a full-out commitment of every part of our beings to live for God. Jesus didn't just sacrifice his pinky toe. He gave everything. We're being encouraged to do the same as living sacrifices. And it starts by not conforming to the ways of this world, but instead"—she points to her temple—"by being transformed up here by the Word."

"Everly, can I add something?" Rebecca speaks up, phone in hand.

"Of course."

"I looked up the word *conform* from Romans 12:2 in the Greek on my Bible app, and it means to fashion ourselves after something else. And the word *transform* means to be changed or transfigured. The example they give is a caterpillar transforming into a butterfly."

"Look at you guys," Everly says. "First, everyone's shy and now we have Greek scholars in here. I love it. Rebecca, you mentioned 'fashioning ourselves.' That sounds like clothes. Which is interesting because fashion is constantly changing. Kind of like the world. If we're always trying to fit into what the world picks out for us, we'll be endlessly chasing different standards. So, instead of conforming, how does it say we become transformed?"

I chime in. "By renewing our minds."

Everly seems surprised to hear from me. "And how might we do that?"

"By reading God's Word and doing what it says instead of what the world tells us to do."

She shows hints of being impressed, then stands up and walks over to a white board where she writes *Renewing the Mind* in black. Under that, she puts a bullet point and writes out *Read and Believe God's Word.*

She turns back to us. "What else? What else did you get from this chapter that might relate back to renewing the mind and not conforming to the world?"

Others start pitching ideas. Ten minutes later, we have four bullet points on the board:

• Read and Believe God's Word
• Recognize Your Identity in Christ
• Practice God's Presence
• Perform with God's Love

"Are we happy with these four?" Everly asks, to the agreement of everyone.

"Alright then, until we meet in two weeks, I'd like us to focus on the first bullet point, which is reading our Bibles every day and renewing our minds to God's Word. I do want to emphasize that it is *us* who renew our minds. Just because we're Christians doesn't mean we automatically think perfect thoughts. We have to put God's Word in our minds and let it live there if we want to truly see a transformation. I also recommend limiting what we take in from the world, too. Social media and all that. I'll send out an email to the group about our next meet-up. Thanks for coming everyone."

Chairs rustle as I go to take a photo of the whiteboard.

Everly photo bombs it. "Hey, a couple of us are going out for a bite. Want to join us?"

"I would, but I gotta study for a statistics test tomorrow. Waited till the last minute. Next time, for sure."

Slight disappointment slips through her poker face. "Next time."

Chapter 05

MONDAY, SEPTEMBER 23, 2019, 8:10 A.M.

THE SUN BREAKS THROUGH the curtains unannounced like a lazy Sunday morning. Except it's Monday. Somewhere along the snoozes I must've hit stop, but it's not stopping my test from starting in 20 minutes. I snatch my backpack and baseball bag and blaze out the door right into rush-hour traffic.

All eyes are trained on me when I open the classroom door. The thudding in my chest is palpable. I walk to the front of the room to grab a test. My watch flashes 121 bpm, and I look up to catch Fallon's playful wink. Not funny. The test looks foreign as my eyes race up and down for something easy to start on.

Slow down. You're here now. One question at a time.

I reach in my backpack—no calculator. It's still at home sleeping on my desk. Heart rate now at 141 bpm and flashing *Breathe*.

No point in saving face now. Like a sheep being lead to the slaughter, I approach the professor and ask if she has an extra calculator. She tells me I'm fortunate we learned to calculate everything by hand. My second walk of shame. I rush to make some sort of progress but am distracted as student after student turns in their test.

Just as I'm ready to give up and hand in a half-answered test, a fluorescent pink TI-84 Plus calculator appears on my desk. I don't look up. Fallon's deep blue nail polish glides along my skin, giving me goosebumps as she passes. I wait until she's gone before sliding the lid off. A small folded note flutters to the ground. I quickly step on it and manage to make some headway with the calculator's help before the professor signals that my time is up. The rest of my classes are a blur and bleed into practice.

2:30 P.M.

Walking into the clubhouse, I hope the music will drown out the negative voice gnawing at me all day since the test.

"Jacky boy, you got a bully today," Coach Jenkins yells through a break in the music.

Not a good day for a bullpen. I empty my pockets into my locker to change for practice when my hand meets the slip of paper. I study the outside of Fallon's note and make sure Tim's not around before opening it. *Your cute when you're nervous. Maybe you'll study with me next time:)* Her phone number is at the bottom. I fold it and return it to my pants pocket before rubbing my face in my hands.

Out on the field, the air is dry and stale, finally showing hints of fall. *What about that note? She wants you. Shut up. Focus.*

"Jacky boy, let's go," Coach Jenkins calls from the bullpen. He tosses me a ball and I rub the laces rapidly against my palms. He instructs,

"Five pitches in a row to the corners before movin' on. You catch too much of the plate, start over."

He calls for the catcher to set up a mannequin in the right-hand batter's box to make it more game-like. After I warm up, I signal to my catcher that we'll focus on low and away to a righty first. My first pitch paints the black.

"Good," Coach Jenkins says. "Anybody can do it once though. Let's see it again."

I succeed in hitting my spot again before missing over the plate with the next.

"See ya ball," Coach shouts. "Start over."

He moves on to the other pitchers as I take a deep breath and begin again. Five pitches later I'm starting over for the fourth time, missing badly in the dirt and again out over the plate.

"Make an adjustment, Johnson," Jenkins hollers. "Can't keep making the same mistakes."

Back turned to the catcher, I again move the ball between my palms. *What are you gonna do about that note? You can't tell Tim. When are you going to talk to your dad? You should probably do that soon. What about Everly? She's cute. Loves God.*

"You gon' stand there all day or throw the dang ball?"

I toe the rubber as my catcher sets up low and away for the umpteenth time. The ball sails up and in. *Whack.*

"Down goes the mannequin. Down goes the mannequin," Coach Jenkins yells, drawing everyone's attention. "Boy . . . I don't know where your head's at today but it certainly ain't here. You take your butt in that clubhouse, do what you gotta do, and come back a different ball player. You hear?"

"Yes, Coach."

In the clubhouse, my glove slams against my locker. My best pitch yet. I crash onto the clubhouse couch, soaking in the weight of the day. I close my eyes and focus on each cleansing breath. In through the nose . . . hold . . . release . . . empty.

After a few rounds, Mack's voice arrives: *See your heart in your hand. Now slow it down. You tell it when to beat. What light are you in? Red.*

What light have you been in all day?

Red. Deep red.

When did you notice?

Just now.

Thwack! Coach Jenkins swings the clubhouse door open, disrupting my quiet time. "What in the hell be goin' on in your head, son?"

"A lot."

He hobbles his way over and plops down on the couch across from me. In a softer tone he says, "When you walk in this locker room, you gotta be able to separate your personal life from your performance. Leave that stuff at the door. It ain't gonna help you none out on that field. We all got life going on, but right now we can't do nothin' about it but be where we at. You gotta be here, son."

"I know."

He climbs to his feet and raises his volume. "Knowin' is only part of the equation. The doin' is where it's at. When you ready, I see you back out there."

The door closes and I go to my locker to review my performance routine game plan. Soon, Mack's voice returns: *Strive for five with your release point. Make sure you're in green before you toe the rubber. See your target and tell yourself what to do. Then allow yourself to do it. Compete with what you have. No excuses. Wash. Rinse. Repeat. Compete.*

When I return to the bullpen, my command of the strike zone shows up. It's not pretty, but Mack's words cement my routine and focus, helping me to check in after each pitch.

"Much better, Jacky boy. Much better," Coach Jenkins says. "Whatever pow-wow you gave yourself in that clubhouse did you some good. Next time come out like that in the first place, ya hear?"

"Yes, Coach."

"You wanna play pro ball, you gotta be able to separate that personal life from your performance."

Coach's words trigger the conversation back in Mack's office on the day of the funeral: *If you're going to fully focus on the draft . . . it might be worth it to get some answers so it's not eating you up inside.*

One thing at a time. It's time I have that talk with Dad soon.

Chapter 06

FRIDAY, OCTOBER 25, 2019, 4:45 P.M.

A MONTH FLIES BY, AND it's already the Friday before Halloween. Coach gives us a surprise weekend off, which works in my favor as Dad and I have dinner plans for the first time since I helped him move into his new place four months ago.

After class, on the way to his place, I blare my car music, trying to drown out the latest round of 21 questions with myself:

How are you going to bring up the divorce?

What's he going to say?

How will he react?

Are you sure you want to know the truth?

Maybe you should wait until the next time you see him.

No, you need to get this off your chest.

Then, a phone call through the car speakers. It's Tim.

"Come out with us tonight, bro!" His speech is already slurred. "It's the Halloween beer pong tournament."

Then Fallon's voice chimes in. "Yeah, Jacoby. You promised you'd come! Tim's dressed up as Popeye, and I'm his sexy Olive Oyl."

I laugh. "I would guys, really. But I'm having dinner with my dad tonight. You have fun, though. Sounds like I'm missing out."

"Come over after dinner then," Fallon insists.

"Leave the man, alone," Tim says.

I check my mirrors as I exit for Dad's new place in Huntington Beach. "If we finish early enough, I'll try to stop by. If I don't, make sure you take some pictures."

I've gotta see her in that Olive Oyl costume.

"We will!" Fallon says.

5:49 P.M.
Dad's new place, Huntington Beach, Ca.

I pull up to Dad's condo and wish I hadn't. Not that I don't want to see him. I miss him. I just don't want to mess things up between us. It's weird knocking on a door where your dad lives and not walking right in.

"Good to see you, son." We hug. His scruff scrapes against my cheek. "How was traffic?"

"About an hour to go 20 miles."

"Not bad for a Friday." We laugh.

His dress shirt is partly unbuttoned, revealing a wife beater undershirt and patches of graying chest hair. Rough day, maybe. Maybe a rough couple of months.

In his cramped kitchen, take-out Italian pasta, garlic bread, and salad are ready to go on the table. We catch up on life and the first half of Fall Ball—surface talk for 45 minutes about what Mack and I are working on and the struggles and triumphs all on display in front of scouts. And of course, how bad the Angels were again this year.

"You full?" Dad asks after I decline another serving.

"Yep. Your best cooking yet."

"I thought so, too." An old smile surfaces as he clears our paper plates. "I know it's not your mom's cooking . . ."

I've downed my water three times, yet my mouth is still a desert. I refill my glass at the fridge dispenser and stare at a picture magnet of him and me from my first year of Little League. Life and baseball were innocent then. We sit back down and he sips the remains of a beer. My conscience gnaws at me like a dog on his bone.

"So, what's on your mind, son?"

"Nothing."

"I know that look. What's going on?"

I shuffle a bit in my seat and try to meet his eyes. "I guess I'd like to know what happened between you and Mom."

He takes a long swig of his beer, finishing it off. "I thought that might be why you drove out here."

He leans back in his chair, opens the fridge, and pulls out another beer. The sharp snap of the bottle cap twisting off and rolling across the table captivates me.

"What'd your mom tell you?"

My eyes remain on the red bottle cap. "She said to talk to you."

Silence. I peek up, but he too is eyeing the bottle cap.

"Jacoby, I don't think now's a good time to discuss this. You don't need any more distractions from baseball right now."

"This *is* distracting me from baseball. No one's saying anything."

A long pause. "You're not going to want to hear it."

"Just tell me."

"Fine." He takes another swig. "I cheated on her."

It doesn't register in my head right away but my face is already burning. Then, the meaning of his words pummel me. I scoot my chair away from the table. Away from him. "You what?"

"It's complicated, and I haven't sorted it all out."

"Seems simple enough! You slept with someone who wasn't your wife. That wasn't my mom."

He says nothing. A floodgate of questions rush my mind, but the only thing one that breaks through is: "Are you still seeing her?"

Hesitation. No answer.

"Are you?"

"Yes."

"Why?"

His fist makes the table jump, and the bottle cap drops to the floor. "Because she pays attention to me, Jacoby. Your mother and I were on the rocks for a while. She was always too busy. Too tired. So, I found someone who wasn't."

"Just like that, you gave up on 20 years of marriage? And me?"

"I'm not discussing this with you right now. I did what I did and I'm doing what I'm doing. End of story."

A Nolan Ryan fastball straight to the chest. No backing down. No remorse.

"You're unbelievable." I slam my chair back against the cupboards and make for the door. "At least Mom had the class to let me hear it from you."

I speed off down the street. *And I was worried I'd be putting him out? My whole life he wants to preach commitment—school and baseball. School and baseball. No distractions. That's how you'll get drafted. All the while he's out screwing someone? Screw him. Hypocrite.*

"Siri, call Mack." Straight to voicemail. *Come on, Mack. I need you right now.* I hang up. It's past 10 p.m. on the East Coast. Probably sleeping. Suddenly, I don't want to go home. I just want this all to go away.

"Siri, call Tim!"

Several rings let out through the speakers before Fallon's wobbly voice picks up on Tim's phone through the party music. "Jacoby!"

"Hey, where's Tim?"

"Please tell me you're coming over to Bauer's. Tim's passed out drunk and people are writing in Sharpie all over his face. He was my beer pong partner. I need you here."

"The beer pong tournament's still going on? Trust me, you don't want me as a partner. I've only messed around with water cups before. Never beer. Plus, I haven't had the best day—"

"What do you think alcohol's for? It'll make you forget anything. Just get here and be my partner, okay?"

I blow out a forceful breath. *Sexy Olive Oyl.* "I'll be there in 20 minutes."

7:43 P.M.

Bauer's backyard is lit up by flood lamps with EDM music penetrating my chest as soon as I step out of the car. I enter the backyard at the side gate where Natty Light and PBR cans litter the grass like land mines. Several teammates, along with the softball girls, push their way in and out of the sliding door, sporting neon tank tops, trying not to splash their beers.

"Jacoby!" Bauer shouts above the voices and music, kicking away a few silver cans impeding his path. He puts his arm around me, smelling of booze and sweat and something else. "We need you to play, bro. Tim's passed out, and Fallon needs a partner."

"I heard. I'd really rather just watch."

"Nope. She needs you, man. Pretty much everyone else already got knocked out of the tournament."

He forces a full red Solo cup into my hands, sloshing beer onto my shirt. He quickly lays out the rules of beer pong. A ping pong table without a net is staged for a team of two at each end where red Solo cups are arranged like bowling pins. Toss a ping pong ball into a cup, and the other team has to pull that cup and drink the inch of beer in it. The first team to have to pull all their cups loses. If at any time a player shoots a ball into an opponent's beer in hand, it's an automatic win.

Bauer raises his cup to cheers me. "Got it?"

"I guess so." As the others cheer me on, I take my first sip. *So that's what bitter beer face means.* I take another. *Still pretty bad.*

We mob to the backyard where Fallon's filling her cup at the keg. "Ready to win?" she asks, handing me a firm slap to my backside.

Dang, she looks good. "Let's do this." We clank cups and sip, never breaking eye contact. "Does all beer taste this bad?"

"This is the cheap stuff. It's not meant to taste good. Just meant to get you drunk." She winks. "I'm glad you came."

"Where's Tim?" I yell over the music.

"Who knows. Passed out somewhere. Serves him right. He started drinking way too early." She hands me two ping pong balls and points to the cups at the other end of the table. "You should take some practice shots if we're planning on winning this thing. Everyone else is drunk so we should be okay."

When action starts, our opponents Greg and Ashley get off to a quick lead, making the same cup on their first shots, requiring us to not only pull the cup they both made, but two additional cups, and give them balls back. Fallon makes me chug the three cups. After that, we battle back and forth, Fallon making all of our cups.

Finally, I make a cup, splashing it in without hitting the rim. *There we go.* After each team uses their one re-rack and make a few more cups, we're somehow in a showdown with one cup each remaining.

Ashley, having missed her shot, cheers Greg on as he steadies himself with one hand on the table and takes aim. It looks good from release, hanging in the air in slow motion before toilet-ringing around the inside rim. I'm frozen. Then, Fallon instinctively bends over and blows it out of the cup, still dry, saving the game.

The crowd erupts in response as she presses her body against mine in an ecstatic embrace. A good portion of my beer spills on her, which she Zamboni's right off her arm, not wasting a drop. We're a shot away from knocking off the number-one seed. Across the table, Ashley and Greg are doing their best to distract us, throwing out insults and shaking butts and boobs. It doesn't matter though. The liquid confidence is having its effect on me. I'm locked in. Unshakable.

The crowd around our table triples in size as word spreads of the possibility of us knocking off the one-seed. Fallon encourages me with another firm smack to my backside. With a hushed buzz in the air and the stench of sweat and cheap beer, I de-grass my ping pong ball in the water cup and flick it dry. With softened elbow and rhythmic knees, I release it into the air with magnetic arc and a bucket full of confidence. The feather-light ball splashes down center cup and the backyard erupts. Fallon jumps into my arms and kisses my cheek. Game over.

Ashley and Greg reluctantly congratulate us. "Good game, rook," he says, refusing to look me in the eye. Disgusted more at himself than with me, I'm sure.

While waiting for the next game to finish to see who we play in the championship, Fallon and I head for the garden hose on the dark side of the house to hydrate.

"Good time with your dad?" she shouts over the music.

"He's been cheating on my mom." *Wow, that came out easy.*

"What?"

"My dad. He was cheating on my mom."

She pulls me closer, and I yell into her ear. The closeness feels good. Right. I can barely make out her face. Then I feel her lips on mine.

Pull away, Jacoby. Pull . . . away. But I don't.

After a moment, she pulls back and wanders back to the crowded beer pong tables.

What the—?

Since no one's around, I use the corner of the backyard fence as a bathroom and take out my phone, almost fumbling it. A text from Everly lights up my screen from 30 minutes ago.

How's your Bible reading going?

I laugh. I've got bigger things to deal with than reading a Bible.

Me: Is ths a Christian booty call?

A minute passes before three little dots pop up.

Everly: Haha. No. Just seeing if you'd seen anything cool in your reading.

Me: Haven't read. Thins arn't great rit now.

Everly: Everything ok? Want to read together tomorrow morning?

Me: Sre

Everly: Awesome. Coffee shop on Harbor Blvd near campus? 10 am?

Me: See yo there.

Everly: Looking forward to it. And I'll teach you how to spell:)

I scroll through my texts. Yikes.

All of the sudden, the music cuts out.

"Ladies and gents," Bauer starts in. I zip up my pants and head back over. "Welcome to the championship between the number-sixteen seed, Jacky boy and Fallon, versus the number-four seed, me and Eva."

Everyone's got their phone out to potentially film beer pong history. Across the beer pong table, the mirage of cups dance as I recount what just happened on the side of the house. I turn, and Fallon is already inches from my lips. She signals for me to come closer.

"I like playing with you," she whispers in my ear, running her hand up my neck and through my hair.

I bathe in the moment before pulling away slowly, remembering everyone's got their phones out. "Let's win this."

As the championship gets underway, the liquid jacket of PBR paired with adrenaline numbs me from the dropping temperature. But Fallon and I begin to look like a true sixteen seed. When she finally drains our first cup, Bauer and Eva have only two cups remaining. It's all but over when I slosh my ping pong ball around in a grassy cup of water and scour their cups for a willing receiver. Just before I shoot, Fallon whispers in my ear about the rule Bauer had mentioned regarding a player who makes a ball into the opposing player's beer cup in hand, automatically wins it for their team.

I hold the edge of the table and wait for Bauer to be momentarily distracted. I don't have to wait long before he leaves his cup unprotected. I try to hide my excitement as I fake aiming for the cups on the table and shoot for the red Solo cup in his left hand.

Plop!

Unaware, Bauer sips his beer and is met with a wet kiss from my floating ping pong ball. Game over. The crowd recognizes my genius play and rushes Fallon and me, pressing us together from all sides.

In the midst of the scrum, I feel Fallon's light blue eyes inside me and her seductive lips trapping me and pulling me in.

07

SATURDAY, OCTOBER 26, 2019, 10:43 A.M.

I WAKE UP IN MY own bed with a throbbing hangover.

A familiar fragrance rattles my memory. I roll over and see Fallon's bare back. *What did I—we—do?*

Tell me I didn't just blow 19 years of smart decisions on one drunken night? My briefs on the floor all but confirm it.

Tim. I reach for my underwear and scramble out of bed to my door, clinging to the wall for balance. The throbbing in my head is exploding, bringing Tim's open door in and out of focus. He's not home. Thank God.

I nudge Fallon softly at first, but her snoring remains in rhythm.

I nudge her harder.

"Stop."

"You gotta get up. Tim could be here any second."

"I don't care."

"Did we . . .?"

"Yes."

Silence pummels me. I grab hold of the wall again as acid seeps in my throat. "Are you sure . . . ?"

She rolls over. Her black eye makeup is smudged like a drunken clown. "You really don't remember?"

"I don't want to. You gotta go. Tim can't know about this."

She rolls back over. "He'll be fine with it. Him and I aren't together."

"I'm serious, Fallon." I throw her *Olive Oyl* costume on the bed. "You gotta go."

"I'm not wearing that home. Give me some basketball shorts and a shirt."

I fling open a drawer and toss some clothes on the bed I won't miss. "Get out so I can change."

In the living room, I search window to window for Tim's car in the parking lot. *Please don't come home. Please don't come home. What's taking her so long?*

Fallon finally emerges in my clothes, costume in hand, with traces of faint red and black makeup. Without saying a word, she grabs her purse and keys and slams the door. *I guess that's how I got home last night.* Immediately, sweat hits me. A foul acid pours into my mouth before I can reach the toilet.

A bit later, I crawl back in bed next to Fallon's expired perfume and pull out my phone to check the time. It's 10:52 a.m. with 7 percent battery life. There's a bunch of missed texts, including three from Everly. I totally forgot about her.

9:50 am: Hey I'm at the coffee shop a bit early. What can I get you?

10:10 am: Just making sure we're still on for studying today

10:23 am: Maybe another time. Please text me you're safe when you get this

I plug my phone into the wall and turn it face down.

3:26 P.M.

The front door shutting startles me out of sleep. My heart rate picks up as I remain perfectly still under my sheets, expecting him to rush through my door and beat the crap out of me. Instead, the bathroom door closes and the faucet flows. I hop out of bed to open the window and spread cologne to mask Fallon's perfume. The bathroom faucet finally ceases, and Tim's door closes. I fall back asleep.

It's night when the microwave beeps. My stomach forces me out of bed.

"Hey," I say, walking into the kitchen without making eye contact.

Crack! I stub my toe and almost knock right into Tim.

"Evening, tiny dancer," he says. "I heard you did mighty well last night."

What's he talking about? "I guess we won. At least I think we did."

"I heard you made it in Bauer's cup for the win," he says, like a proud papa.

I'd forgotten. "Lucky shot."

"How'd you get home? Your car's still at Bauer's."

Stop interrogating me. "Honestly, I have no clue. I don't remember much after the dog pile."

He laughs. "After these nachos, I'll take you over there to grab your car."

"Thanks." We briefly exchange eye contact for the first time. He still has faint evidence of Sharpie marker on his face and arms from last night. "Looks like they got you pretty good."

"Bastards." He shakes his head before turning to pull nachos out of the microwave. "Been trying to wash it off for hours. Kick a man while he's down."

Then sleep with his girlfriend. "Hey, I'm good just taking an Uber to my car. You don't have to drive me."

"I'm happy to do it. My roommate has his first hangover."

After Tim drops me off at Bauer's, driving home is the first sober thing I do all day. The second is to text Everly.

I'm alive. And really sorry.

She replies a few minutes later.

Glad. Saw you on Instagram. Hope you had fun last night.

I flip through and watch a short Instagram video showing me and Fallon with beers in hand. The post already has hundreds of *likes*.

That sinking feeling returns. This can't be good.

Chapter 08

THURSDAY, NOVEMBER 14, 9 A.M.

THREE WEEKS AFTER THE beer pong tournament, phantom burning and itching continued to eat at me to where I couldn't shake the idea that I might've contracted something from Fallon. I skipped a class Tuesday morning to get tested at the student health clinic. The rest of Tuesday and yesterday, I rotted in my own mental prison thinking that I might have the clap or some other STD.

I skipped another class again this morning to receive my results. In the clinic waiting room, I thumb through Instagram, looking for a distraction. The door to the exam room finally opens.

"Mr. Johnson?"

Of course she's smokin' hot. And judging me by my chart for

having some incurable disease, probably. All because of one frickin' night. I'm lead by the physician's assistant to a small room and sit on the paper-covered examination table while she silently reviews my chart. I wipe off my hands on the paper sheet several times.

"Mr. Johnson, we ran your bloodwork and urine through our comprehensive 10-test panel for sexually transmitted infections. Fortunately, tests came back negative for the more serious STIs like HIV and hepatitis that stay in your system forever. However, you did test positive for chlamydia."

My face is burning. A quiver in my voice. "What is that? It's curable, right?"

"It is treatable, yes."

She pulls out a prescription pad and scribbles. "Chlamydia is a common bacterial infection in sexually active people your age. Over three million people contract it every year without ever showing any symptoms or feeling different. But it's important you get on the antibiotics immediately or it may cause health problems later."

"Absolutely."

She continues to scribble. "I highly recommend remaining sexually inactive until you've completed the two-week medication cycle. For the future, using condoms greatly reduces the risk of contracting STIs, but of course, abstinence is the best way to stave off any sexual risk whether infection or pregnancy."

Why is she so robotic about all this? This is my life we're talking about, lady.

"I also recommend you contact your sexual partner. Since you marked that this was your first sexual experience, it would benefit this person to know they have chlamydia. If it is a female, and she goes untreated, it may very well cause her to lose the ability to have children in the future."

"I'll tell her." I emphasize the *her*, just to be clear. "Thank you."

While at the student pharmacy waiting on my prescription, I figure Fallon is still in class and I can get away with leaving a voicemail. But part of me doesn't want to tell her at all. Part of me wants to let her find out on her own or never. Part of me doesn't want her to ever be able to have kids. She took something from me I can't ever get back and left me with a little something extra to remember her by. Alas, my conscience wins out. *She's not all to blame. And I owe it to Tim.* Fortunately, she doesn't pick up and I leave a voicemail.

When my prescription is filled, I immediately wash down the recommended dose. *If only I could wash away everything that happened. Never again, Jacoby.*

2:32 P.M.

At practice, Chainsmokers radio crowds the clubhouse once again as I'm on the mound for the start of today's intrasquad game. With each piece of street clothing I take off, I try my best to drop a distraction, and with each piece of practice gear I put on, I try to button up my focus. Coach Jenkins comes by my locker and informs me that Coach Hill wants to stretch me out to four innings today or 90 pitches, whichever comes first, for my last start of Fall Ball.

When I'm done changing into my practice gear, I dig my laminated pre-game routine out of my baseball bag and review it.

Goal: Throw one quality pitch at a time.

Pre-Pitch Process:
1. *Agree on sign.*
2. *Big breath.*
3. *Visualize ball trajectory to glove.*
4. *Challenge statement (pitch and location) with proper tone (use demanding voice with hard stuff or soft voice with soft stuff).*

Post-Pitch Process:
1. *Deep breath.*
2. *Ask: Green, yellow, red?*

3. Get back to green before toe hits rubber (breathe, positive self-talk, recall past success, or act it till you feel it).

PS: May never feel it but don't show it. Not everything will go your way. Embrace the suck. Win the mind and you'll be fine. Rinse, repeat. Compete.

I return the list to my locker and lay on the clubhouse couch. The music drifts away as my focus moves inward to my toes, then my feet, and my calves, squeezing then releasing. My quads, my hamstrings, and my glutes—squeezing and releasing.

Mack's voice fills my head: *Feel the difference between tension and relaxation.*

My arms, deltoids, biceps, triceps, and my forearms, squeezing and releasing. With my hands, I make a 50 percent fist . . . then 80 percent . . . then a 100 percent, squeeze and release. Dead silence and darkness. Then up the back of my neck to my forehead, pulling my eyebrows up to form wrinkles. Squeeze, squeeze, and release. Squint the eyes . . . and release. Clench the jaw . . . and release. A thin river of drool dribbles down my cheek as my jaw parts and my tongue goes limp.

In my mind's eye, I'm on the mound. The crunch of my spikes pierces the mound's damp clay. Huge body language, calm and confident, narrowing in on the catcher's sign. A lefty steps in. Just a body. Fast ball away. My two-seam fastball starts down the middle and tails low and away from the hitter. Trust it. Good. Get the ball back, breathe, check your signal light, green, repeat. One pitch at a time.

A faint voice calls to me like someone talking underwater. "Jacoby, you okay?"

Another voice in the distance chimes in. "Leave da man alone with his thoughts, gosh dang it."

Aware, but not listening, I finish off two more batters before taking two deep breaths, wiggle my toes, and flutter my eyelids, returning to the clubhouse music. *Own it out there. You've seen it in your mind's eye. Now go do it in real life.*

They weren't Mack's words anymore. They were mine.

Out on the field, to the delight of the scouts, I'm sure, I cruise through the first three innings nine up, nine down, including six strikeouts, one dribbler infield hit, which was quickly erased on a double-play, and a chopper back to me that I jogged over to first for the out.

Finish this last inning strong.

In the fourth inning, they're back to the top of their lineup, starting with our starting center fielder. A scrawny lefty with wheels. Bauer puts down his pointer finger and taps his left inner thigh for a fastball away. I grip a two-seamer. *See the path to the glove. Fastball away.*

"Steerike!" Coach Jenkins yells behind me.

Nice spot. Deep breath. Where you at? Green. Go. Bauer calls for the same pitch.

"Strike two!"

Way to repeat. Deep breath. Where you at? Green. Go.

Fastball up. Way up. The hitter doesn't bite. Now it's 1-2. Bauer wants a curve ball. I shake him off. *The batter's expecting it.* Two-seam fastball in. *Start it as his hip, work it back over the plate with just a touch off.*

Pang! A bleeder up the first baseline.

"I go," I call out. I barehand the ball off the grass and flip it to first base. One out.

I strike out the number-two hitter on four pitches, but then serve up a jam shot to our best hitter, who muscles it over the second base-men's glove. The next batter chops a ball to short, but Tim boots the grounder. Two men on, two outs. I surrender a walk on borderline pitches to the number 5 batter, loading the bases. Coach Jenkins is squeezing me. Good.

Breathe. Embrace the suck. One ground ball away from getting out of the inning.

Bauer calls for a curveball first pitch. *Ping*! The batter pulls the ball down the third base line where the third baseman moves behind the bag to field it. The ball ricochets off the bag and into left field.

Gotta back up home plate.

Two runs score. I get the ball and walk back to the mound as if I had just struck the guy out. *You did your job. It's out of your control. Win the next pitch.*

The seven-place hitter's up next, a pudgy right hander, with runners now on second and third with two outs. I wipe the sweat from my forehead with my sleeve. He works the count to 2-1 before a cement-mixing curveball has him out in front of the swing. He chops the ball to Tim at shortstop and is retired at first. Three outs.

"Jacoby, hold up a second, now," Coach Jenkins calls to me. He puts both hands on my shoulders and with Halls minty breath tells me, "That didn't look too pretty at the end there, but you just got a little unlucky. You was dominant for three innings, lookin' like that first rounder I heard we was gettin. Keep yo' head up, son. Lots of good things to build off. I watched for some kinda body-language from you when things went bad, anything—but you didn't even flinch after none of dat. That's what I'm talkin 'bout. Big difference from when you done first arrived. Mighty fine, son. Mighty fine."

After practice, Coach Jenkins informs me Coach Hill wants a word. I walk into his office and settle in across from him, next to Coach Jenkins.

"Coach Jenkins and I were discussing your last few outings. Quite an improvement. Maybe not on paper, like what happened today, but it's Fall Ball and I'm not as worried about results. The good news is that you're velocity is increasing and your breaking stuff is sharp. That's what we're looking for. Keep it up and you've got a good chance of starting for us come spring."

"Thank you, Coach."

Awesome. It's happening.

Mack's the first person I text with the news, then replay my four innings of work on my drive home, recalling what went well, what could've been better, and what I'll do in practice this week to improve my pitching. Everything seems to come back to throwing one quality pitch at a time. One step closer to the bigs.

After my shower and protein shake, I can't find my phone. I throw on my sandals and a shirt to search my car. It's in the center console. I tap the screen. Two missed calls, a voicemail, and a text. All from Fallon.

I play the voicemail. "I got your voicemail. Thanks. Call me back. We need to talk. I've been sick. I might be . . ."

Chapter 09

MY MORNING ALARM BEEPS, but I don't need it.

Pretty sure I didn't sleep at all.

This happens to other people. Not me. There goes the draft. Bye-bye baseball. Hello McDonald's.

By the time I reach the campus parking lot, I've pulled up Fallon's number five times but can't bring myself to call her. Finally, almost without permission, my trembling thumb taps the screen and *Fallon . . . Calling Mobile* appears. The loneliest rings in the world.

"Hey," comes from a sunken voice on the other end.

"Hey, Fallon."

"Why didn't you call me back last night?"

"I . . . I just couldn't. How, or I guess, when will you know for sure?

"Today after work."

"If the test is positive, are you sure it's mine?"

"Either yours or Tim's."

I say nothing for a while. "Did you tell Tim anything?"

"I told him to get checked. Nothing else."

"Okay. Will you—can you let me know when you find out later?"

"Yeah."

"And if you need anything let me know."

"Thanks. Bye."

2:30 P.M.

Just before practice begins, Coach Jenkins meets me at my locker to tell me Coach Hill wants to see me again.

"Close the door behind you, Jacoby. I got a call from the Athletic Director this morning about a video on social media that surfaced a few weeks ago. Seems he just got wind of it. Something to do with you drinking at a party."

He slides his iPhone across his desk to me. "Anything you want to tell me before we meet with the AD? He's expecting us."

"Coach, that's the first time I've ever drank. I swear. It won't happen again."

"I believe you. And I hope it's only a slap on the wrist, but whatever the AD says, goes. Unfortunately, I have no power in the matter."

We walk to a building I've never been in and wait for the secretary to escort us through a door that has *Mr. Wade* on a name plate with *Athletic Director* underneath.

"Come on in," the AD says. He makes small talk like he's actually interested in getting to know me before we get down to the issue at hand.

"Listen, Jacoby, at OCC we have a no-tolerance drinking policy for any underage athlete. No matter how good." He acts like he's on my side. "That being said, there's evidence that's been brought to my attention of you drinking on the weekend before Halloween. Do you deny it?"

Deny evidence? Who is this guy?

"No."

"Then this puts me in a tough bind."

"What are my options?"

"There aren't any options."

"Then what's the bind?"

"Jacoby, we have to suspend you for the last week of fall practices and the first five games of the spring season."

My eyes close in disbelief. One drunken night haunts me again. "Who else?"

"What do you mean?"

"Who else is getting suspended? I can't be the only one?"

"The evidence only clearly shows you and that young lady."

"Are you serious? The whole team was there."

I shove my chair back and start to leave before Coach Hill grabs my arm and tells me to sit down. "We're on your side, Jacoby. The dean wanted to kick you out of school after seeing that video go viral. It's a reflection on the college. Mr. Wade went to bat for you and got you a reduced suspension. You should be thanking him."

I meet eyes with the AD. "How does the dean even know who I am? I've never met him or you and yet you're deciding my baseball career?"

"You decided your career by going to that party," he says.

"How am I getting suspended for something that didn't even happen on campus? I've *never* heard of someone getting in trouble for something this small. Be honest, would this happen to any other athlete at OCC?"

"We did the best we could," the AD says.

"That's what I thought," I say. "You'd put me on a pedestal in the school Hall of Fame if I get drafted next year and you'd use my name for recruiting for years to come, but now you're just trying to save face. Really went to bat for me, didn't you?"

This time Coach Hill doesn't try to stop me from leaving.

Back in the locker room he tells me I can't even be at the field until my suspension is up. But he didn't say anything about the weight room. Before clearing out my locker, I change into my workout clothes in hopes that Sarge is in the weight room. The gym door is unlocked when I arrive. Inside, fans are blasting as he works out the volleyball team. Everly is drenched in sweat, doing box jumps. She peeks up, and we briefly meet eyes before she continues her jumps. I walk backwards to head out.

"Johnson, start on the foam roller," Sarge shouts. "I'll be with you in 10."

I slink over to the warmup area, put my earbuds in, and face away from the volleyball players. A few minutes later, there's a sharp kick to my thigh. Everly stands over me. Her sweat drips to the mat.

I take out my ear buds. "Hey."

"No practice today?"

Something like that. "Long story."

"I see. Are you coming to G2G Sunday? Haven't seen you in a while."

"I figured you wouldn't want me there."

"Everyone's always welcome." She walks backwards towards the door and flashes a playful wink. "I won't hold my breath, though."

I deserved that.

"Johnson," Sarge yells.

I put my foam roller away and tell him about the suspension. He doesn't ask questions. Over the next hour, he punishes my body with battle ropes, wall-balls with rotation, back squats, front squats, deadlifts, weighted lunges, and whatever else he could conjure up. After the workout, he helps me off the mat and we walk outside.

"So, what's your plan?" he asks.

"I don't know. Hang out here I guess."

"That's a start. You think an apology to the dean will do anything?"

"Doubt it. Not sure I'd do it anyway."

"What'd I tell you earlier this year? Everyone's gunning for you.

Comes with being a big shot."

"I'm sick of people calling me that. I'm sick of the expectations. Being under everyone's microscope. I just want to be me."

"The *you* I met two months ago didn't drink."

"Yeah, well, maybe you'd have done the same thing if you found out your dad cheated on your mom." I look away.

He puts a hand on my shoulder. "I'm sorry to hear about your parents."

"I don't need a pity party."

"No pity parties. But it doesn't mean I can't feel for you. If you can't be at practice, then commit to being here the rest of Fall Ball. I'll get you ready for season. But if I hear about any more drama, don't even bother showing up. I don't got time for that. Deal?"

"Deal. Thanks, Sarge."

On my way back to my car, I have two texts. One from Bauer saying he's sorry to hear about what happened with the suspension. The other from Mack checking in on me. I'll call him tomorrow. I call Bauer. He's having a few people over later but if I want to swing by for a few minutes to blow off some steam, I can.

5:27 P.M.

Bauer's sitting on his front steps when I arrive, squinting through the last bit of sun, beer in hand.

"My man," he shouts, already buzzed. We wander to the backyard where two lawn chairs perch on the back porch overlooking the ping pong table, where three weeks ago all my troubles began. I explain to Bauer what happened with the Athletic Director leading to my suspension.

He ratchets open the cooler and slushes around in the ice water to fish out can of PBR for me. "That sucks, man." He tries to hand me the beer.

I wave him off. "That's what got me into this mess."

He sets it by my chair and pulls a baggy from his pocket, lighting up a joint until it's crackling. "You were supposed to get drafted out of high school, right?"

"Yeah. Probably just lost my chances of getting drafted this year, too."

"Dude, it's just a five-game suspension. It just takes getting seen one time by the right scout."

"True."

Bauer picks up the beer next to me and puts it in my hand. "I'm telling you, a beer is the best cure when you're feeling down. You'll be smiling in no time."

The can numbs my hand. *Could be nice to numb the mind a bit, too.* Bauer raises his beer to cheers me. *Screw it. One beer won't hurt.* "Fine." I crack it open and cheers him.

"Good man."

Another swig goes down even easier. "Between baseball and Fallon—"

"Wait?" Bauer drags his lawn chair closer. "Fallon?"

Crap.

"What about Fallon?" he pries. "Did you guys hook up?"

"No."

"You guys totally hooked up!"

"Dude . . . shut up," I tell him. "I didn't even mean to say anything."

"It's cool. Your secret's safe with me."

I chug my beer. A faint buzz sets in. A byproduct of not having eaten anything all day. Soon enough, a smile begins to surface for the first time in days. We sit in silence for a while as Bauer puffs away at his joint. When the sun is gone, Bauer pops the cooler top again and slides another can beside my lawn chair.

"Round two's even better," he says.

"I'm good for now."

"Wuss."

I shake my head at his egging me on. "You know what?"

I crack open the ice cold PBR and guzzle it. In the overgrown backyard grass, now under nightfall, the lonely beer pong table begs for company. I finish my second beer faster than the first, set it down, stomp it flat, and frisbee it across the backyard into the weeds. "How can I get suspended for something that didn't even happen on campus?"

"They don't care about us, but I got your back." Bauer words are starting to slur. He heads to the side of the house to turn on the flood lamps that light up the beer pong table.

We continue talking for a while as the evening chill rustles through the backyard trees. The beer pong table all lit up only reminds me of Fallon. "I think I'm gonna head out."

Bauer returns to his lawn chair. "Stay bro. People should be here anytime."

"I'm good. Not trying to party." I feel for my keys, cell phone, and wallet.

"If you get pulled over and the cops find even a drop of alcohol in your system, you're done. I got a DUI last year. Thought I was good to drive. The cop and a $10,000 fine said I wasn't. I still don't have my license back yet."

"But you drive all the time."

"It ain't illegal unless you get caught." He laughs before it turns into a series of heavy coughs.

"Yeah, good call." I settle back into my chair. "So, you used to live up in the Bay Area, right? Is that where you're from?"

"I'm from here, actually. My parents split up a couple years ago. My mom left my dad. I don't blame her. He was always traveling back and forth to the Bay Area for work. He's in the tech industry and made out pretty well with a couple startups. I moved up to the Bay with him after the divorce. But when I got that DUI, my stupid coach kicked me off the team, and my dad threw me out. So, when I moved back here, he bought this house as an investment rather than step up and be an actual father."

"Wait, you own this place?"

"Yup." Bauer grabs me another cold one. "Well, my old man does. But I'm the king around here."

I crack the can open and raise my can to cheers him. "To deadbeat dads."

He laughs and downs his beer. "Dude, you're already three beers deep, why not just stay the night? It'll be a couple hours until you're totally good to go, anyways."

Sounds logical. "Better safe than sorry."

"My man!" He takes a final deep puff of his joint before stomping it out under nightfall.

"What's on your bracelet?" he asks.

I swivel my wrist. "A Bible verse I like."

"What for?"

"I forget it's even there most of the time."

"What's it say?"

I hate to even read it to him. *You sure are living the gospel aren't you, Jacoby?* "It says **Phil 4:13**: *I can do all things through Him who strengthens me.*"

"Yeah, you can do all things except play baseball for a while."

We both laugh. I don't know why. It's not funny. *What am I doing here?* The guilt pushes me to drink more. A few beers deeper my walls topple, and I vent to Bauer about my situation with Fallon and Tim. Soon after, a bunch of people start mobbing in.

For the next hour, a few of us play beer pong. The night time chill has no effect on my liquid jacket. I reach my favorite status, buzzing hard enough to where I can't get the smile off my face. To keep the buzz alive, I head for the fridge to grab another brewsky.

Empty. "Bauer, we're outta beer."

He storms into the kitchen more than buzzed. "What do you mean we're out? The party just started." He searches for his keys. "I'll be back."

"Dude, never mind. We're fine. It's not worth it."

He turns on me, booze oozing from his pores, eyes blood shot. "We're good when I say we're good. Are you coming?"

"I'm ... I'm gonna sit this one out. But I'll be here when you get back."

Just like that, Bauer shoves past me. "Lame. You guys are all lame."

The screech of his tires down the road are a signal to the rest of us to resume the party. I continue my quest to keep my buzz afloat. Then, the front door swings open and Fallon, dressed in high rise jeans and a shirt revealing no signs of a bra, strides in. She spots me, her aroma swirling inside me. I want to hate her but, right now, I don't. Can't.

"Hey, you," she says, six pack of longneck watermelon IPA's in hand.

"Fallon." My disgust melts quicker than butter on a hot pan.

"Bauer texted me to come over."

"He did, did he?" *That son of a . . .*

She pulls out a longneck brew and hands it to me. "You shouldn't be walking around empty-handed."

I grab it and twist off the cap, wishing I could put up more of a fight. We clank our bottles.

"Can we talk somewhere?" she asks.

We go down a hallway to a quiet room.

"I'm not pregnant, Jacoby."

I close my eyes, smile, until I laugh. "Are you sure?"

"Yeah. I took it twice to be safe. Both negative."

"Good." I turn to leave, but she grabs my arm.

"I'm sorry, Jacoby. What I did—we did—I shouldn't have done that to you when you were drunk. I just . . . I just want a nice guy. I deserve a nice guy. And when I heard you might be going pro, I guess I wouldn't have minded getting pregnant."

Seriously? "I don't do that stuff. I'd never done that, and I don't remember any of it. And you did that just so you could *maybe* have a kid with me?" I wash down the faint taste of battery acid with the watermelon IPA.

Fallon puts her hand to her mouth, "Wait . . . you're . . . you're a virgin? I mean, *were* a virgin?"

I take a swig, trying to mask the heat wave sunning my face, then walk out of the room. "Enjoy the party."

The music blares in the kitchen where teammates are pouring vodka into five shot glasses glued to a ski. "Jacoby, we need you," Greg says. Without hesitation, I head for the vacant fifth slot. *Gotta celebrate not being a baby daddy in eight months.*

In unison we yell, "One . . . two . . . ski . . ."

It goes down smooth without it's normal bite. The warm liquid moves through my body like a masseuse working the tension out of my forehead, neck, and shoulders. I gotta pee. I head for the bathroom. Hovering over the toilet, I unzip with one hand while unlocking my phone with the other to view a missed text from Everly.

How are you? I hope you can make it to G2G Sunday night:)

I try to text back one handed and almost fumble my phone into the toilet. Better to pocket it.

In the hallway, the music pulls me back toward the party. One hand tracing the wall for support. A voice from the bedroom I was in earlier calls to me and a hand pulls me into a dark room, followed quickly by familiar intoxicating lips meeting mine. Any traces of bitter acid were washed away with the ski shot.

Fallon and I trip in the dark, landing on the edge of the bed and knock heads before crashing to the ground laughing. No pain. Numb. The ground is as suitable a spot for us as any. Clothes are coming off. I hear yelling and slamming doors in the hall but ignore the noise. Now it's closer. It's fine. We're invincible. I'm invincible.

Then, our door almost swings off its hinges as the light reveals us.

"What the hell," Tim's voice booms. He stands over me, and my heart hides in my throat.

"Tim. This—

"Save it."

I scoot away from Fallon in search of my shirt while she scrambles for a blanket to cover up.

"He brought me in here, Tim. I swear."

The battery acid returns at the sound of her voice. She doesn't dare show me her eyes.

"She's lying Tim. I was minding my own business in the hallway when—"

Bam!

Tim's fist sends me to the ground, and yellowish purple constellations take flight. "You deserve each other."

I lay there, eyes closed with the room spinning, head throbbing. "Did you at least use your left hand?"

"Shut up. I know what happened between you two. I was going to let it slide as a drunken mistake. But here you are returning to your own vomit. I want you out of the apartment by Monday."

He leaves. Trailing off, he says, "Bauer was right. He said tonight would be unforgettable."

Chapter 10

THE SKIN IS TIGHT where my face used to be. Out of my right eye, I put together that I'm still at Bauer's, as last night comes flooding back: Fallon. Tim's fist. Kicked out of my apartment.

My left hand searches along the carpet for my phone until they meet under the bed. A blurry 8:03 a.m. or 8:08. I stagger to my feet, allowing enough time for the room to stop spinning. The hallway is littered with beer cans all the way to the kitchen, where a lipstick-stained pint glass with the remains of vodka-something remind my stomach of that ski shot. But it'll have to do.

In the living room, a few scattered bodies lie passed out. Bauer is nowhere to be found. The slider to the backyard is already ajar. The morning air is bitter cold in the shadows and quickly whisks away the toxins sweating from my pores. The beer pong table lays dormant among the weeds. *This isn't you. What has this place gotten you?*

"Mornin' bro." A random guy comes around the side of the house, struggling to buckle his belt. He reaches into his pocket for a little baggy.

"Morning."

"Pretty crazy night last night. Did you see that fight? Wait—"

He comes closer, blowing smoke out of the side of his face. "You're the guy that got knocked out. Man, your face is messed up."

"I deserved it."

"Was she worth it?"

"Nope."

His laughter turns to an uncontrollable cough. "Who cares, right? We'll do it all over again tonight."

All over again tonight . . . all over again . . . all over again.

"I don't think so."

I can no longer stand the glass's vodka stench, so I water the grass and go inside to grab my wallet and keys. In my car, after some fuzzy brainstorming, I'm left with one choice. Drive to Mom's, explain everything, and ask if I can move in for who knows how long. On my drive over, a call comes in through the Bluetooth speakers. My vision is still blurry.

"Hey, Mom."

"Mom?" A male voice rings out. "It's Mack."

Hang up. Hang up. Hang up.

"Hey, Mack. Sorry. I thought it said Mom. I got your text yesterday but was busy. I meant to text you back."

"I was just checking in. When I don't hear from clients, typically things are either going so well they forget to reach out or so bad they're too embarrassed to talk to me. So which is it?"

I signal at a four-way stop and fight the windshield glare with my good eye. There's no use lying. "I'd like to say the first one, but that wouldn't be true."

"Is everything okay?"

"I messed up." I pause, my voice welling up. "Pretty bad."

"Jacoby, there's nothing you could say that'll change my opinion of you. We've all messed up. Trust me. I've heard it all and done it all. Just tell me how I can help."

Several blocks pass. I zoom through a yellow that may have turned red while still in the intersection. A car leans on the horn confirming my trespass.

"Are you driving right now?"

"Yeah. Headed to my mom's."

"Pull over when it's safe."

I swing a right turn into a fast food restaurant parking lot. "Alright, I pulled over. Mack, I don't know what to do."

"Slow down. Take some deep breaths and gather yourself. I've got all the time in the world."

A minute passes and my head is glued to the steering wheel. "I don't even know where to start. I thought I was fine and then I woke up this morning and everything hit me."

"What do you mean?"

Another big breath. "I got kicked out of my apartment. There's a lot to it, but I gotta be out by Monday. I'm heading to my mom's house right now to figure things out."

"Does she know you're coming, yet?"

My fingers fork backwards through my hair. Head throbbing from either the booze or reality, I'm not sure. "No. I'm calling her when we get off the phone."

"Don't call her. Hang tight. I'll call you right back."

Within minutes Mack rings me. "Do you remember how to get to my house?"

"I think so."

"You're going to go across the street to my neighbor's house. His name is Frank, and he'll have a key with instructions waiting for you in his mailbox."

"Wait, what?"

"You're moving into my house, Jacoby."

"I can't . . . No Mack. I don't deserve it."

"I'm not saying you do. But I have a house and you have a need. It'll be a good place to get a fresh start."

"Seriously, I can't do this."

"It's not going to protect you from any danger you bring on yourself, but if you're serious about getting back on track, then I trust you in my home."

The levy of tears finally breaks. I mute the line, and the interior of my car shakes until I take my hands off the wheel.

"Jacoby, are you there?"

I try to sturdy my voice. Then I unmute the line.

"I'm here. I'll take it. Thank you, Mack. For everything."

10:47 A.M.

When I pull up to the curb, I hardly raise an eye at Mack's house. As promised, an envelope addressed to me sits inside Frank's mailbox across the street. I retreat to my car.

Jacoby,

Call the moving company below. Everything's paid for including the tip. Just tell them where to go. The guest bedroom and bathroom across from my office are yours. Make my home your home. Frank will be by tomorrow morning to give you the lay of the land. Call me after. Much love in Christ, Mack.

I place the letter on the passenger seat and dial the movers to meet me at my old apartment. *Tim, please don't be there when I get there.*

When I arrive, Tim's bedroom door is open. He's not home. *Thank goodness.* His baseball bag lays open in the middle of the living room next to the coffee table covered with more used-up joints than a Bob Marley concert.

How am I no better than this guy? In the kitchen sink, a mountain of moldy cereal bowls is stacked to the brim, and the trash can pleads to be dumped. I box up my few kitchen and bathroom belongings as quickly as possible. Soon, a moving truck beeps while backing up into the apartment complex. The movers, a couple of guys my age, take care of the furniture in my bedroom. When they carry out my mattress, I'd rather they just burn it. Everything's out in one haul. Before I leave, I make sure the dishes are washed, the burnt joints are trashed in the dumpster, and Tim's baseball bag hangs on the balcony getting some fresh air. I leave the key on the mantle along with a sticky note. I take one last look and exhale slowly before closing the door.

4:30 P.M.
Mack's House

When the movers finish unpacking my things at Mack's house, I thank them and close the door, still watching their blurry figures fade through the glass paneling. Must be nice dropping off people's baggage and walking away free of it. Mack had once told me that's what happens when we pray. When we drop our baggage onto God's shoulders, He is much more capable than we are to bear it.

My back slides down the wooden door to the cold tile. The skylights and floor to ceiling windows borrow the late afternoon sunlight to illuminate the yellow, orange, and blue walls. I put my head between my knees ...

God, I messed up. I don't deserve this house. Or Mack. Or his generosity. I don't know what's happened to me. Please, please forgive me. I want to be back right with You. I tried to take the world on by myself. My Dad. Fallon. Baseball. What a joke. You are what I need. I lost sight of that. But I see it now. With one good eye, at least. I know You're always looking out for me. Thank you for blessing me with this house and with this new start. Please bless Mack big time. You are so good to me and I don't deserve it. But I will do my best to make the most of this new opportunity. I need You. I love You. In Christ's name. Amen.

When my head finally rises some time later, the once loud walls are dark. I feel my way through the foreign house to my bedroom and flick on the light. In the guest bathroom, I hardly recognize the kid staring back at me. I move close enough to the mirror for my nostrils to spray hot air onto the mirror and suck it back in. *This isn't you. Get back on track.*

I turn out the light, climb into bed and slip away.

SUNDAY, NOVEMBER 17, 2019, 9:47 A.M.

A faint knock at the door jostles me from my deep REM sleep. Then another, much louder. I open one eye. Still blurry. I feel for my face. A little less puffy than yesterday. At the door, Frank, Mack's neighbor, is tall with gray curls, a sagging face of weekend scruff, and a slight belly atop a pair of khaki shorts.

"Welcome to the neighborhood, Jacoby," he says, with a firm handshake.

"You must be Frank?"

"I try to be."

I squint.

"It's a lame joke," he says. "Sometimes it works. Rarely, actually. Anyways, Marcus said you'd be around awhile, so let me show you the place."

He gives me the layout and shares that he's been close neighbors with the Macks for over 30 years. They'd vacationed together and shared a Bible study for the past 20 years on Wednesdays nights. We end our tour back in the kitchen, where he turns down a glass of water in lieu of returning to his own lawn chores. When he leaves, I phone Mack.

"Good morning, Jacoby." His clear voice seems to have no recollection of my faults. "All settled in?"

"I really appreciate this."

"Glad to do it. Did Frank show you the place?"

"He did. Nice guy. Interesting."

A quick chuckle comes through the phone. "So you've heard his jokes?"

"If that's what they were."

"He's a good man, and Doris is wonderful as well. She and Suzie were very dear friends."

"Your house is awesome."

"Yes, we—I like it." He pauses. "I need to get Suzanne's mother to an appointment so I'll be brief. I didn't have you move in just to hand you a bunch of do's and don'ts. That would be a contract. Not a gift. But I will ask you to be smart in who you invite over to the house."

"Of course."

"I'll share a little something and you can take it for what it's worth. I once worked with an elite female gymnast. She was only a freshman in college when she qualified for the Olympic Games. Every time we talked, I'd remind her to read 30 minutes of God's Word daily no matter what the day brought. It would be a way of always keeping God's wisdom close amidst the chaos constantly bombarding her.

"Pretty soon her popularity skyrocketed with all the hype of the Olympics, and some of her roommates kept pushing her to party. Everyone wants to party with a celebrity. She was reluctant at first and kindly rejected their offers. But they were persistent and kept hassling her. What do you think eventually happened?"

"She gave in."

"Sure enough. Anyone without a firm foundation will. Partying became more attractive than time spent with God until finally her Bible got shuffled under homework and other school books. Years later, she admitted to me it got to the point she'd go weeks without spending any time in God's Word or remembering to pray. When one goes, the other tends to dwindle, too. Anyway, she told me one time that she cleaned her desk and found her Bible. She said shame kept her from opening it. And guilt kept her from praying. At some point, she became numb to both."

Sounds like someone I know.

"She said her biggest regret was missing out on the joy of competing with God while part of the Olympic gymnastics team. I told her God never left her. She said, 'I know . . . I left God.' It was evident in her performance at the Olympics."

"What do you mean?"

"She allowed the big moments to get to her—the crowd, the expectations, the sponsors, the pressure—whereas before she was dialed in competing with joy for an audience of One."

"At least she made the Olympics."

"True, but she could have had so much more."

"So you want me to read my Bible for 30 minutes every day?"

"I want *you* to want to read your Bible every day. When you're consistently reading about Christ's life, you can't help but become more like Him. You become what you look at. For good or bad. I want you to love God for you. For you, Jacoby."

I run my free hand through my hair, considering his words and the last few days. I'd bitten the lure of Bauer's lifestyle, the house, Fallon, the parties. But it was all meaningless. Fun in the moment? Sure, a bit, but everything I was trying to escape is still there, waiting for me. Nothing's disappeared.

"I'll find my Bible and do the reading. For me."

"Good. Have you been attending that campus ministry?"

"No. There's one tonight but—"

"Be there."

"Okay. Can we get back on a regular talking schedule?"

"I'm here for you when you need me. One last thing about the house . . . If you want Internet, you'll need to call and set it up. That'll be the only thing I'll ask you to pay."

"I'll take care of it if I need it. Thanks again for everything. Talk soon."

I go to the bathroom and study my black-and-blue eye. *It starts tonight at Bible study. A new you. Even with that face.*

Chapter 11

SUNDAY, NOVEMBER 17, 2019, 7:07 P.M.

G2G Meeting on Campus

IARRIVE AT CAMPUS MINISTRY. Car still running.

Leave, Jacoby. You're already late anyway. Do you want to explain to 20 people about your face?

My car door interrupts the lies. Bible in hand, I head inside. Everly is already into her opening prayer as I weasel my way to an empty seat in the circle. She finishes and everyone in unison mumbles, "Amen."

"Alright," she begins. Her bright smile latches onto eyes around the room. Even mine. "I can't believe we're already halfway through November! In our last few meetings, we've been emphasizing reading our Bibles daily. I hope it's becoming a lifestyle for each of you."

Reading? Read my black and blue face and you'll know how much I've been reading.

"As I was doing my preparation for tonight, I was reminded by my mentor that renewing the mind is not automatic just because we're Christians. Unfortunately, we don't just get a new brain. We still have the same brains, same habits, and same lifestyles as before. The only thing that changes with being Christian, is that, we now have the *ability* to renew our minds to God's Word and maintain a new standard of living and thinking. I have an example that should make this concept come to life that I'll share in a minute. Can anyone remember what the four parts to renewing the mind are? Just shout them out if you have one."

"Read your Bible," someone says, to the amusement of everyone.

"I hoped we'd at least get that one. What else?"

"Recognize . . . something, something, something," a soccer player blurts out to more laughter. "I remember the word recognize at least."

Everly helps her out, "Good start. Recognizing your position in Christ. Good. What else?"

"Practice God's presence," Connor says.

Everly's eyes widen with each response. "And the last one?"

"Performing with God's love," someone adds.

"Very good. Reading the Word, recognizing our position in Christ, performing—wait, I mean, practicing God's presence, and then performing with God's love. Whew, try saying that five times fast."

Chuckles move through the circle.

A hand shoots up. "Everly, why do we keep calling it the *renewing* of the mind instead of just the renewed mind?"

"Great question. The *i-n-g* in renewing emphasizes an ongoing process, whereas renewed kind of sounds like a one-and-done action. We never arrive. It's a constant re-upping with God's Word because the world is constantly throwing stuff at us. That'd be like giving yourself one bit of positive self-talk on the field and thinking you're set for the whole game. What happens if—well, *when*—things go wrong? We need that constant positive self-talk. We need to do that with God's Word, too. Let's turn to our theme verse, which is Romans 12:2. I'll be reading out of the NIV."

I leaf through my neglected Bible pages, and my lips curve up on their own. *This feels right. These are my people. The family of God.*

Everly begins reading the Scripture. "Do not conform to the pattern of this world, but be transformed by the renewing of your mind. Then you will be able to test and approve what God's will is—his good, pleasing and perfect will.' We kind of talked about this when we first met, but let's invest some time looking at what it means to conform and transform. We'll start with conforming. It's nice to get the bad stuff out of the way first."

Light laughter.

"Conforming isn't a passive act where the world lays it on you without your permission. I always think about us in big game situations where we might be persuaded to fear, or be nervous, or feel pressure. But no situation can force you to feel anything without your permission. It's our job as athletes to control our thinking in each situation. Would you agree?"

Most of us shake our heads while a few hold blank stares.

"The world works similarly. It cannot force you to do or feel anything without your permission. It's our responsibility to choose whether we're going to conform to this world or be transformed by God's Word. The first part of our theme verse might better be translated, 'Do not conform yourself to this world . . .' It's an active doing. Not passive. Think about your favorite athletes. Maybe how they wear their uniforms or style their hair. If you choose to emulate any of those athletes, that's you choosing to conform yourself to that style. Make sense?"

Mental light bulbs go off around the room.

"Now, I'm not saying you can't aspire to be like your sports heroes. It's just an example of conforming. We live in the world and tend to conform to the world sometimes without knowing it. It's subtle that way. But no one changes our minds except us. We are the bosses, the coaches, of our minds. God's Word says we aren't to conform ourselves, that we aren't to imitate, participate, or associate with the ways of the world . . ."

Well, haven't I just been the poster boy for conforming to the world of late?

Everly's words come back into focus. "It's we who choose not to conform and choose instead to be transformed. And how do we become transformed?"

"By renewing our minds," a few people mumble softly.

"By what?"

"Renewing our minds!"

Everly gets a kick out of that. "Right. So, I have an analogy I think will help us understand the importance and value of renewing our minds daily with God's Word. With all the demands we have with our sports and lives, how would we be doing if we only ate once a week?"

Giggles.

"We'd be in pretty big trouble to say the least, right? Take a moment to consider your spiritual nutrition. Maybe you are full, maybe you're just getting by, but maybe you're starving."

Connor, the lanky cross-country runner sitting next to Everly, is a spitting image of my spiritual body.

"I hate to say this"—Everly slowly scans the room—"but if we're only squeezing a few minutes of God's Word in per week, we're going to be spiritually weak. You see what I did there?"

A few laughs. *I got it.*

"If we're not feeding on God's Word, then we're feeding solely on the world. The ramifications are just as detrimental to our mental lives as going weeks on Rice Crispy Treats is to our physical bodies. How much time do you spend living off the junk food of the world?"

Too much.

"Think of all the food we have in our cafeteria that's screaming for our consumption. Some of it's healthy, but most of it's not. It takes mental effort to go with the healthier choices. But we never regret it when we eat the good stuff. How do we feel when we eat well?"

"Strong," someone shouts. Then others chime in.

"Light."

"Energized."

"Clear-headed."

"Sad." Everyone turns to the speaker. "Yeah, I'm talking about when my friends are scarfing down pizza right next to me."

This sends everyone into hysteria. *Right on.*

"That's true," Everly says, reigning in the group. "But at least you don't have to deal with the carb coma later. Do you see what I'm getting at, though? In life, there will always be something seemingly more appetizing than spending time reading and studying God's Word, but nothing could be more satisfying, fulfilling, and fruitful to our spiritual and mental growth. We have to eat it until we come to crave it, and then we become transformed by it from the inside out.

"We have to get to the place where we truly care about what we are feeding our minds. How often do you go on social media or watch TV and feel better afterwards? I personally have never gotten off social media and felt better about myself. Maybe you have. On the flipside, I've never closed my Bible after reading and felt it was a waste of time. I don't think I'm alone in experiencing that. That's what I have for you tonight. I hope it encourages you to go to the Scriptures more often. Anyone have anything to add?"

Rebecca, the softball player, chimes in. "It's crazy how different the way of the world is from God's Word. I'll be reading my Bible and my roommate will be like, 'Why are you even reading that?'"

"Yeah," a gymnast agrees. "It's weird. It's like it's almost a good thing, though, when that happens because then you know you're doing something right. If the world isn't calling you out, we're not sticking out."

My conversation with Bauer about my bracelet comes back to me.

Everly chimes back in, "And it's so easy to get sucked into the world, isn't it? It's all around us constantly. That reminds me, can we flip to one more verse in Job 23?"

Furious pages flip around the room. Except mine. The beer pong tournament, Bauer's sweaty head lock, the night with Fallon—all take turns beating me up.

Everly begins, "In Job 23:10-12 it says in the NIV, 'But he knows the way that I take; when he has tested me, I will come forth as gold. My feet have closely followed his steps; I have kept to his way without turning aside. I have not departed from the commands of his lips; I have treasured the words of his mouth more than my daily bread.'

"Most of us are familiar with the life of Job. Even amidst all the physical and mental adversity he dealt with in his life, he continued to treasure God's Word more than the physical food that sustained him. It was his reliance on God that helped him endure great tragedy and still come out on top. God hasn't changed. Neither has His Word. When we rely on it and value it more than our daily food, it will sustain us and help us withstand every temptation and every trial. If you don't believe me, find a promise from God's Word and put it to the test. That's what renewing the mind is. It's a continuous cycle of receiving God's Word, retaining it in our hearts and minds, and releasing it through our words and actions. Receive, retain, release. Then rinse and repeat as needed. Okay, I promise I'm done this time."

Her face beams as everyone claps.

Dang, she knows her stuff. No way she dates a guy like me. She probably prefers guys like Connor over there.

Everly seems to remember something and raises her hands to grab our attention. "Thank you. God's Word is great. One more thing. For these next few weeks as we begin to look at recognizing our position in Christ, I want you to consider what it means to be a Christian and what it means to be a Christian athlete. The benefits, maybe some of the costs, and how you are currently living out your Christian identity both on and off the field, okay?"

Christian identity? I'm not even sure I still have one.

A few people scribble in their notebooks while others start stacking chairs. I try to sneak out to avoid any questions about my face. Outside the building, I hear a voice.

"Jacoby," Everly says through the crisp night air.

"Hey," I say to the ground. *Almost got away.* "Thanks for teaching tonight. I needed it."

She moves closer to me under a street lamp. "I did too." She moves even closer. Investigating. "Now I see why you're leaving so fast."

"What?"

"Your makeup looks terrible. If you need help, just ask next time."

A smile grabs my face. It hurts so good. "Will do."

"So, when are we hanging out?"

I kick around a few leaves. "You still want to hang out after I stood you up last time?"

"Make it up to me then."

"When?"

"How about now? The chairs are stacked. I just need to lock up. Meet me at Roll 'n Scoop in 10 minutes?"

"Didn't you just get done talking about all this healthy—"

"And now I want ice cream. Sue me."

Was that an Office reference? "At least I'm not the only hypocrite at G2G."

"Will frozen yogurt ease your guilty conscience?"

"Ice cream sounds good."

She holds her smile on me as she walks back towards the door. "I'll meet you over there in a bit."

9:13PM
Roll 'n Scoop

Strawberry, birthday cake, peanut butter, and mint chocolate ice cream chill the air. I pull out my phone in a pink corner booth while

I wait for Everly. *No social media, remember?* I pocket it. A couple, my age, probably on their second or third date, are holding up the line to share taster spoons. Everly walks through the door, and I meet her in line to scope out the flavors.

"I got this." I slide my debit card.

"Well, in that case, let me top this off with more gummy worms and Reese's then."

"I'm pretty sure you can't fit anything else in that cup."

"Don't tempt me with a good time. Ben and Jerry are my best friends come finals week."

We sit in the corner booth where she holds up her ice cream. "We should probably ice your face with this."

"Funny."

"You have a good story to go with it?"

I start in on my toppings, chewing a gummy worm. *What version do I tell her?* "Let's just say I haven't been reading my Bible much the past month."

"Every streak starts somewhere, right? Who was that baseball player that hit in all those consecutive games?"

"Joe DiMaggio. Fifty-six straight. Back in 1941."

She devours a bite and licks her spoon clean like a five-year-old in heaven. "Beat Joe's streak then." We occupy ourselves with our ice cream.

"I didn't think you'd come tonight," Everly says.

"Why's that?"

"I've been hearing . . . things."

"What kinds of things?"

"Gossip."

"I love gossip."

She stabs her ice cream again. "I don't."

"Whatever you heard is probably true."

"It's not my business." She chops at a Reese's chunk. "I just want to make sure you're doing alright."

"I'm good. And you're right. I almost didn't show. That little negative voice."

Her eyes grow inquisitive. "What made you come then?"

"How many guys do you know with a black eye who don't need some Jesus?"

She laughs and pushes her nearly empty cup to the edge of the table as if telling the remaining bite that she got the last laugh. "I know that voice you're talking about."

"Nah, that's not possible."

"Ha! Trust me, I'm quite human despite what you might see once every two months."

Brain freeze. Brain freeze. "Hold on." I feel like she's looking at Sloth from the *Goonies*.

She reaches over and squeezes my forearm. Her touch somehow eases the throbbing, but I keep up the act a bit longer.

She releases my forearm. "I have a negative voice, too. We all do. I call it—well actually—the Bible calls it our 'old man nature.' We're born with it due to Adam's sin, and the deceiver's always talking trash and telling us we're not good enough. He knows what makes us tick and what ticks us off."

"My old man's been pretty convincing lately."

"And you've been believing him?"

"Up until tonight, yeah. Do you talk to yours?"

"I try not to. The Bible says to consider him spiritually dead. Would you talk to a dead person trying to belittle you?"

Good point.

"There's good news, though." She says. "It's our new man nature. When someone becomes a Christian, he or she gets a new nature. When Christ died, the Scriptures say our old man died with Him. When God raised Christ from the dead, we were raised with Him and received the new man nature when we became a Christian. The old and new man are talked about in Ephesians and Colossians quite a bit." She pulls out her phone. "You should download this app called

Parallel Plus. You can have like four Bible versions up at a time."

"I have that app. My mentor suggested it awhile back."

"It has this version I really like that simplifies things called *A Journey through the Acts and Epistles Working Translation*. WTJ for short. Here it is."

She comes to my side of the table and scooches in close.

"Ephesians 4:20-24 says, 'However, you did not learn about the Christ in that manner, inasmuch as you heard of him and were taught about him, even as the truth is in Jesus, namely, that you strip off the old man according to the former manner of life, which is corrupt according to deceptive cravings, and that you be renewed in the spirit of your mind and that you clothe yourselves with the new man, which was created in accordance with God in justness and devotion to the truth.'"

"Sounds like changing clothes again," I say.

"Exactly. We're doing the taking off of the old and the putting on of the new."

"Seems simple enough."

"Simple, but not easy. Worth it, though. It gets easier the more we read God's Word."

"Does he eventually go away? The old man?"

"He'll still try to talk to you, but the more we starve him and feed the new man God's Word, the more the old man fades and the new man takes center stage. When Christ comes back and we get new minds and bodies, the old man will be done away with for good."

How does she know so much? "I feel like you already know more about the Bible than I'll ever know."

Her cheeks flush. "It's not so much about what you know but about how much you live it."

I nod. "You want to go for a walk to burn these calories off?"

"That might be a long walk."

"I promise to have you home by midnight to get your homework done."

I hold the door open for her, and she grabs a jacket from her car. We stroll a bit in a comfortable silence, watching the car headlights pass.

"When did you decide Christianity was for you?" I ask her. "Were you raised in it? Or did you pick it up on your own?"

"Kind of both. I was raised in the church but definitely took it for granted early on. I dated a guy the last two years of high school who wasn't really into the Word, and I just kind of stopped reading my Bible. I still prayed here and there and went to church occasionally, but I wasn't pursuing God."

"What happened? Not with the guy. What changed, I mean?"

"My grandma." Her lips part, revealing joy. "She took me to breakfast at our favorite spot and basically told me to get it together."

"Your grandma told you to dump your boyfriend?"

"Basically." Our shoulders brush against each other in passing strides. "She saw potential wasting away and had the heart to tell me. She was my best friend."

After a comfortable silence, I recommend to her that we turn around. She obliges, and we head back toward our cars.

"Well . . . Did you break up with that guy?"

She laughs. "Yeah. I did."

So you're saying there's a chance!

"It's been nice having this last year to just grow with God and help others," she says.

Or not.

"Leading G2G keeps me accountable, and I really do love sharing God's Word. I just want to live it bigger each day. Or I should say, allow Christ to live in me more each day." She smiles up at me. "So, you ready to start a streak like that Joe DiMaggio guy?"

"I already have today in the books. Tomorrow's day two."

"I'd be happy to study with you if it helps keep you accountable. I could use some accountability, too. You know, if you care to show up." She playfully nudges into me.

"I was waiting for you to call me out on that. I deserved it. And I really am sorry I stood you up."

"I know." She's smiling. I am too.

We walk in silence the rest of the way as the lights from Roll 'n Scoop edge closer.

"This is me." She opens her car door before turning back to me. "We choose how far we want to go with God. If you practice His presence in your life as much as you practice throwing that baseball, I think you'll go far with both."

A tiny speckle in her right eye is wrapped perfectly in honey yellow. I hug her and hold on longer than necessary.

"I think you're right." I pull away. "Hey...do you wanna hit golf balls with me next Saturday?"

Her cheeks turn rosy again. "Don't expect a lot. I haven't played in ages."

"Does 11 a.m. work for you?"

"I'm busy then."

Shot down.

"But 11:01 works."

Dang, she got me.

She's laughing as she gets in her car. I close her door and yell through the window, "Then it's a date."

Chapter 12

AFTER CLASS, I HEAD to the weight room to work out with Sarge. The gym door swings open just as I approach, and he puts his key in the lock.

"What you got for me today, Sarge?"

He shakes his head. "I told you to stay out of trouble."

"What?" My face still shows faint black and blue evidence. "Oh, that. It was stupid. A misunderstanding."

"I laid out the conditions, and you broke 'em. Bauer came in here earlier, and I turned him away, too."

"Why?"

"You didn't hear? He got arrested for a DUI last week. Second offense. Coach Hill kicked him out of the program." Sarge starts walking towards the parking lot.

"Hey, Sarge . . . I'm sorry. Don't give up on me."

"Never said I was. Good luck, Johnson."

At my car, I call Bauer and he fills me in on what happened. We agree to meet up at a nearby park so I can throw and stay sharp.

4:32 P.M.

Bauer drops his truck tailgate where his gear bag and a cooler rest. "What's up, buddy?"

"Dude, that sucks." *Wait. He's still driving his truck? When will he learn?*

"It is what it is, man." He grabs his catcher's mitt and mask.

We don't say much for the next twenty minutes as I throw 45 pitches before it gets dark. We head back to his truck, where he pops open his cooler. "Have a beer with me."

"Nah, I'm good on the drinking for a while." I raise my water bottle.

"Nonsense." He pushes a beer across his tailgate. "It's the least you could do."

"What does that mean?"

"Nothing. I'm just playing with you. I respect that you're not drinking, actually." He cracks open a beer and downs about half of it. "So, after the whole Fallon fiasco, you seeing anyone else?"

"Not really."

"What do you mean not really? You either are or you're not."

I sip my water. "There's this volleyball player. We've been hanging out. Well, once."

"How's she in the sack?"

"It's not like that."

"Well, what are you waiting for? She's a volleyball player so she's gotta to be decent. Have a pic?"

"Wouldn't show you if I did."

"So when are you going to hook up with her then?"

"Dude. We're just friends. Chill out."

"Guys and girls can't *just* be friends. They even made a movie about it."

"Must be true then."

"Exactly." My sarcasm buzzes right over his head. "What's she good for then?"

"She's a great girl. Loves God. She's an athlete so she gets the whole focus and priority thing."

"She needs to prioritize your needs."

"Easy bro," I say, eyeballing him.

"I'm just saying the season will have its ups and downs, and it's nice to have a lady friend around to, you know, help release the tension."

I shake my head. "It's not like that."

"Well, if you keep hanging with her and she's not putting out, you're gonna get frustrated. You're a man. It's biology. But hey, if worse comes to worse, you've always got porn. That never fails to do the job."

"Yeah, porn's not my thing."

"Porn's every guy's thing. Best chicks in the world for free? No risks. No emotions. It's almost better than the real thing. Heck, I'd say it *is* better."

"You go right ahead, big guy."

"You Christians are such sissies. How do you know it's not for you if you've never tried it? All I'm saying is it's there for you whenever you need it. No questions asked. No getting turned down. Heck, porn's more faithful than any girl I've ever dated. It'll take your mind off anything."

I force an appeasing smile and tap the tailgate twice, signaling my exit. "I'll keep it in mind. Not so sure Everly would appreciate me watching that stuff though."

"Everly, huh? The libero in the funny jersey?"

Uh-oh. "That's her."

"It's not like you have to tell her. Girls know we watch that stuff. Heck, they watch it too from what I hear. Besides, it's not lying if you never bring it up."

I start walking backwards toward my car. "It's not my thing, but you go right ahead. Thanks for the bullpen session." *Won't be happening again.*

"Just trying to help a brother out. You got to keep that mind right for the mound so when I take you deep this year, you'll have something to ease the pain."

"You gotta be on a team to do that."

"I got a team. I already got the games verses you guys circled."

"Who are you playing for?"

"Fullerton College took me on. I'm a Hornet now."

"I'm happy for you man. You're a good catcher." I open my car door.

"Two months away. Want to put a friendly wager that I take you deep?"

"You? Hit a home run off me?"

"That's right."

"You're crazy."

"Let's make a little wager, then. I take you deep, and you watch your first dirty movie."

I close the car door.

He jogs over to my window. "I'm kidding. I'm kidding."

He wasn't. I roll down the window. "Tell you what, you hit a jack off me this year and I'll take you to any Ducks game you want."

"Hockey? Fine. But we're going drunk."

"What happens when I get you out?"

"What do you want?" he asks.

I chuckle to myself and shake my head. I ease on the gas pedal. "To be honest Bauer, you don't have anything I want. I'll see you in February."

Chapter 13

EVERLY, DRESSED IN A marshmallow white vest and black leggings, is waiting outside her apartment with a golf bag propped up when I arrive.

"Your own set of clubs, huh?" I put her clubs in the trunk of my black Volvo sedan that definitely needs a car wash.

"They're my mom's." Her smile causes me to smile. "Thought I'd at least look like I know what I'm doing."

"That's half the battle. You should've said they're yours. I would've been intimidated."

"Oh, you'll know after my first swing they're not mine."

We get in the car and drive off.

"Wow, it's clean in here," she says sarcastically. "And that smell . . . is that . . . baseball bag masked in cologne?"

I can't hold in my laughter. "Guilty. I think the stench is permanent. Sorry. I don't go on too many dates."

"Oh, the *date* word." Her vest wriggles against the leather seat, then turns towards me. "It still counts as a date if it's daytime?"

"You don't seem like the friend zone type. So yeah, it's a date."

"I think I just got a little nervous. What driving range are we going to?"

"I'm taking you to my favorite spot where I used to go with my dad. We never really got on the course much. Just hit range balls. We'd go 15, 20 minutes without saying a word. Except when he'd talk in my backswing. Only way he could beat me at closest-to-the-pin."

"Sounds fun. Do you still do that together?"

"Not in a while." Silence. "We're not exactly talking right now."

"I'm sorry."

"It's fine." I turn the radio on low. "So when's the last time you hit balls?"

"Oh, geez, back in spring probably."

"Me too. At least we're even."

"Yeah, right. You're going down, mister."

We park, and I grab both golf bags. I throw a twenty in the machine and it spits out 156 range balls. We head upstairs to the second deck.

"I've never hit from up here before," she says. "It's different, but I like it."

"You can kinda see everything and pick your targets better."

I place her bag on the adjacent 4x4 green turf and divide the golf balls into bins. She selects a club and approaches her ball. Her jet black Under Armour leggings don't disappoint. She must've felt my eyes on her and cranes her head back at me. "Were you planning to check out my butt all day?"

"I was thinking about it, actually."

"Just don't talk in my backswing then."

"Deal." *She's got some sass.*

We hit practice balls for five minutes, not saying much, just laughing at each other with each slice, shank, and whiff.

"What am I doing wrong?" she asks, almost catching me staring again.

"Your eyes. Count out loud a full two seconds after you hit the ball, and I bet it'll still be sailing when you look up."

She tries it. "Well look at you, smarty pants. Maybe you should become a golf pro instead."

"You can't hit what you can't see. I make a living off of batters forgetting that simple step. Well, not a living, yet. Next year maybe."

"Maybe?" She tees up another and whacks it near the 75-yard pin. "Not with that attitude, you're not. So what's this closest-to-the-pin game you and your dad play?"

"Pretty simple. We pick a flag or object like that rusted truck out there with the 100-yard flag sticking out of it. Whoever hits it closer to the location wins the hole. We usually play first-to-ten wins. Wanna play?"

"What are we betting?"

A kiss would be nice. "I don't think it's in your best interest to bet on this game."

"Scared?"

"Fine. Loser buys dinner."

"Who says I don't already have another date lined up later?"

"Better call him up and tell him you're already buying steak for a much better-looking guy. And dessert."

"*And* dessert? Now we're talking."

Everly jumps out to an unexpected 4-0 lead. That's when I take my eyes off her hips and focus up. I win the next 10 straight. She loses with grace and dignity, and I've got the biggest smile on my face that I can't turn off. Not so much because I won dinner and dessert, but because I get to spend more time with her. And, there's no way

Everly's paying for dinner. She watches over the clubs while I run to the clubhouse to get us a couple of hot chocolates. When I return, we cozy up on a bench near the first tee, watching people swing away.

She blows on her cocoa before taking a sip. "So, I don't mean to pry, but why aren't you and your dad talking? You don't have to answer if you don't want to."

"It's fine." I blow away the steam coming off my Styrofoam cup. "He cheated on my mom."

"Oh." A pack of geese fly in the distance above the fairway of hole number one, within range of a golf ball hit off the tee. Her eyes are still on me. "I'm sorry to hear that."

"Don't be."

"When's the last time you talked to him?"

"Last month. I asked him why they split up. He didn't even try to lie or cover it up. He wasn't sorry. He even said he's still seeing the other woman."

"That's awful."

We sip our cocoa in silence. "That's the night I played in that beer pong tournament and got drunk. And why I didn't show up the next morning for our study session."

"I see."

"First time I ever drank. It should've been my last."

"That was your *first* time?"

I smile and turn towards her. "Why are you so surprised?"

"I guess I had you pegged differently."

"Nope. Baseball's my life. Well, was my life. It's still my life. Just not at the moment. I bet you've never had a sip of alcohol in your life."

She laughs. Sips her cocoa. Swings her feet back and forth under the bench. "Let's just say I'm better at beer pong than golf."

"Shut up."

Her pearl whites beam at me. "Maybe you've got me pegged differently."

"Maybe."

"My last boyfriend, the one my Grandma encouraged me to break up with, didn't exactly care for God much, and maybe there were times in my life I didn't represent Christ as well as I could've. If you know what I mean."

"Are you human or something?"

She laughs. "But seriously, I really learned how important it is to be with someone who wants to grow with God together."

"How long were you two together?"

Her face turns away. "Two years."

"Two years! Sorry. I just, I don't get why people stay in things way too long when they know the person's bad for them."

"You've never been in love then, have you?"

"Just with baseball. She breaks my heart every day."

Everly sinks an elbow into my side. "What about you? You've never had a girlfriend?"

"Not really. I talk to a few here and there but I don't like to get attached. I never know where baseball's going to take me." We lock eyes. "You're making me rethink my philosophy, though."

"Is that right?"

"Sure. Who wouldn't go for a girl who pays for dinner *and* dessert."

"Jacoby!"

"I'm kidding. I'm kidding. But seriously, I'm having a really good time with you."

"Good. I am, too. You're pretty good at this for someone who doesn't date."

"You're easy to be around."

We watch another foursome tee off on the number one hole. One of the heavyset guys is wearing red checkered pants. If he's gonna wear those, he better be good.

"Fore!" he yells from the tee box. *Nope.*

"How you doing on that hot chocolate?" I ask.

"Done." She scoops the remaining whipped cream off the edges.

"Me too. Ready to go?"

"What's next? We have to kill some time before that dinner I owe you."

"Don't forget the dessert," I add.

We decide on a movie. *Gemini Man*, starring Will Smith, just came out. During the film, I nudge Everly every once in a while, letting her know I'm near. When the movie's over, I insist on treating her to my favorite hole-in-the-wall burger joint with the best chocolate peanut butter malts around.

"So what about you?" she asks, dipping a fry in her malt. "When you finally do settle down and get a girlfriend, have you thought about what you're looking for?"

To buy some time, I take a huge bite of my barbecue bacon burger with no onions. "I went to a funeral earlier this year. . ." I put up a finger to finish chewing.

"That's random."

"Wait." I finish and take down some malt. "I went to a funeral earlier this year for my mentor's wife. He talked a lot about the highs and lows of marriage and how it was their relationship with God that helped them navigate life together. He said something like, 'It's not about whether I'm right or she's right but about what's right.' He was talking about agreeing on what the Bible says. I definitely want a woman who's humble enough to do that with me. I've hung out with girls who are *never* wrong, and it gets pretty draining."

Her smile tells me she understands.

"He also talked about his wife being his best friend. I'd never thought about it like that until he said it but I guess that's what I'm looking for. A best friend to do life with and have sleepovers with every night."

"I like that."

"But for now, baseball is my baby. The goal next June is to be getting ready for my first summer of pro ball. I say that now, but a lot of things have to go my way this season. I didn't tell you, but that day you saw me in the gym, I got suspended from the team for Fall

Ball and the start of the season."

"I heard."

"Yeah, between that and this"—I tug on my sleeve, revealing my elbow scar— "my draft stock isn't exactly skyrocketing. I'd still say that surgery was the best thing that ever happened to my career, though."

She traces her fingers across my scar. "Why is that?"

"That's how I met Mack. He's my sport psychologist."

She smiles, grabs some fries, and dunks them in ketchup.

"Mack introduced me to the mental game and taught me how to really grow with God. I haven't been doing a great job of it lately, obviously, but he's the one who suggested I check out G2G last year. Where I met you."

I grab some more fries. "What about you? What's the number-one quality you're looking for in a guy?"

"Trust," she says without hesitation. "Trust is big with me. The last guy I dated withheld a lot of things from me, and he always wanted to know where I was."

"Sounds like a jealous guy."

"He was. I want a guy who knows I'm with him and doesn't have to ever worry that I'm with someone else. Otherwise, I'd just rather be single."

"I think that's my favorite part of being single," I say. "I don't have to check in with anyone. Something that I've been thinking about lately, though, is finding someone who can do for me what I can't do for myself."

"Like scratch an itch in the middle of your back?"

"That would be nice, too. But I want a girl to remind me to read my Bible even when I don't feel like it. She would be the real deal for me."

"I like that."

We sit in silence for a bit until we're done slurping down our malts. *I wouldn't be mad at Everly being the one to scratch my back.* When we decide to call it a night, I drive her home and walk her to her apartment door. "I really enjoyed today."

"I did too," Everly says. Her eyes look ridiculously good against the porch light. "Thanks for planning everything out. And for kicking my butt in golf. And for buying me dinner. And dessert. Did I miss anything?"

Kiss her. "Happy to do it. Especially if you're gonna wear those leggings. Just kidding."

"Goodnight Jacoby. Let's do this again soon."

"Definitely."

Our eyes linger. Then she turns to unlock the door.

"Hey, Ev?"

I pull her in close. Her breath is steady and fresh with Wintergreen. Her glossy lips, full and soft, meet mine.

Wow.

Chapter 14

CHRISTMAS DAY 2019, 11:31 A.M.

Costa Mesa, California

I CALL MACK ON MY drive to Mom's house to open gifts.

"Good to hear your voice, Jacoby. Merry Christmas."

"Merry Christmas to you, Mack. How's the weather?"

"Suzie's mother and I are having a beautiful white Christmas here in New Jersey."

"Well, California misses you. We're suffering in this 68-degree blizzard."

"I miss it too. So you're on winter break. Staying busy?"

"Keeping my arm sharp. Been hanging out with this volleyball girl, too."

"Do tell."

"Her name's Everly. She runs the campus sports ministry."

"I like what I'm hearing."

"I'm not sure I'm ready to take things to the next level right before season, but we'll see."

"Who says you have to take things to the next level so fast? Get good at being her friend. The other stuff will come if it wants. Either way be upfront with her."

"For sure."

"What do you like about her so far?"

"She's got these eyes, Mack. They're like little spirals of honey wrapped in hazel."

"Someone took poetry last semester. What about her personality?"

"She's fun. Lighthearted. We've been going to her church every week and she's been coming to the gym with me. I don't know . . . she's just easy to be around. Her relationship with God is strong, and she's been keeping me accountable to read my Bible every day."

"Sounds like a keeper. Good company tends to rub off on us."

"It has. She challenges me. Not a lot of girls do that."

"It's good to find someone who doesn't just agree with everything you say."

"For sure. She calls me out sometimes. I hate it but I love it."

"And you? How are you benefiting her life?"

I let out a single sharp laugh. "Been asking myself the same thing. I'm not sure actually. Sometimes, I don't know what she sees in me."

"Oh, come on. You've got plenty to offer."

"She probably wants some perfect guy who doesn't cuss or whatever. She says trust is really important to her, but there are some things that if I told her, I don't know that she'd want to date me anymore."

"Do me a favor. Go draw a bath and see if your feet hit the bottom of the tub."

"I'm driving. But I get it. I'm not perfect."

"And neither is she. No one is."

"I think we're getting to the point where we'll need to define the relationship."

"Well, you could. That's certainly the world's way of doing things. Why not just get to know the girl with no expectations. Treat her like a sister in Christ and encourage her to be who God's made her to be."

My side mirror is clear to merge over towards my exit. "Yeah. I've been trying."

"That way, whether you two work out or end up just being friends, you've helped each other mature in Christ without any broken hearts due to the physical stuff. And hey, if or when things heat up, just keep your hangouts to public places and keep the fact that she's first and foremost your sister in Christ at the center of it. You can't go wrong that way. Don't feel like you have to be forced into anything. Keep it light."

"I appreciate that advice." I pull into Mom's neighborhood. "How are you doing? How's your heart?"

"God's healing me day by day. I'm just keeping my eyes on the hope. 'It could be today!' as Suzie would say."

I pull up to Mom's house. "That's true. I'm glad to hear you're doing better. I've been praying for you a lot, lately."

"Thank you."

"Well, Mack, I actually gotta get going. I'm opening gifts with my mom. But it's good to hear your voice. I'll call you soon."

"Thanks for checking in. Let me know what happens with this Everly girl. I'll be keeping you two in prayer. Merry Christmas, Jacoby."

11:47 A.M.

Two bulky stockings hang from the fireplace while Mom's favorite Christmas carol, *Deck the Halls,* supplies some resemblance of a normal Christmas without Dad. I place the one gift I got her under the tree. Every year, Mom has a theme, and this year it's "getting back in shape," so I splurged on a TRX home gym. Time for her to get back on the dating scene perhaps.

I walk into the kitchen, arms wide open, with a big smile. "Merry Christmas, Mom."

"Merry Christmas, sweetie." We embrace. "I was thinking we could make some pancakes before opening gifts. Sound good to you?"

"Sounds perfect. I'll help you make them."

"Well, aren't you quite chipper today?" She pours the pancake mix on the flat iron pan.

"It's Christmas!"

Her eyes investigate me. X-ray vision's more like it. "Something's different about you. Are you talking to a girl finally?"

"Who said anything about a girl?"

"You think I don't know my own son? I know it's not baseball season right now, so it has to be a girl."

She can still pick up on my tells. "Fine. Her name's Everly."

She puts down her spatula. "I like that name. How long have you been seeing her? And when were you planning to tell your mother?"

"Slow down. We're just getting to know each other. I'm trying to do things different this time."

"Well, I'm proud of you son." Her eyes are as hopeful as a pitcher staring down zeros in the hit column with two outs in the bottom of the ninth. "When do I get to meet this Everly?"

"Stove, Mom."

"What? Oh shoot." She frantically flips the hotcakes. "You're supposed to be helping me, remember?"

I sip my orange juice and lean into the counter. "I'm sure you'll meet her soon. She's with her family in Big Bear this weekend. She's a volleyball player. We met at the sports ministry last year."

"An athlete and a Christian? I like her already. I think you're being very smart taking things slow. Set the table and I'll bring these over for you to decide if they're worth eating or not."

The pancakes are a bit burnt. But I like them a little crispy. Along with the eggs, bacon, and orange juice, I couldn't ask for a better

Christmas breakfast. "You know what I've never understood," I start in, mouth full of gluten-packed pancakes and fluffy whipped cream, "is how come at restaurants pasta and pancakes are so expensive? I mean, they cost like a quarter to make and they charge a leg and a toe for them."

"You've been doing some deep thinking over winter break haven't you?"

"I guess so. About a lot of things."

"And when will you be seeing Miss Everly again?"

"Probably in the next few days. She's been coming to the gym with me a lot."

"Does she wear makeup to the gym?"

"Wouldn't let her in my car if she did."

"Good. Does she do the selfie thing in front of the mirror? I have the Instagram, you know?"

"It's Instagram, Mom. Not *the* Instagram. You aren't following me are you?"

"You sure like to take those selfies at the gym with that official blue checkmark of yours, Mr. Celebrity."

"That was one photo like three years ago. And no, she doesn't take selfies in the mirror."

"Good. If she did, I could understand you jumping ship. I hate those poses those girls are doing these days."

I reach for the last strip of bacon. "I'd probably leave her at the gym if I saw her take a mirror selfie."

"Jacoby," she says, like only mothers can. "She sounds lovely."

"She is. But with baseball—"

"Don't start up with that. You always look so far ahead and end up scaring yourself right out of every relationship. Just let it be. Let it grow one day at a time and see what happens. If she loves God and you like being with each other, she may be worth pursuing. I don't want you regretting anything while you chase your dreams."

"True." I stand up to clear our plates.

"Honey, don't worry about it. I'll clean up later."

"You cooked. I'll clean."

"If you're set on cleaning up, I'll run upstairs to wrap the last of your gifts."

1:13 P.M.

Mom and I lounge in the living room, drawing out Christmas as long as possible as *Chestnuts roasting on an open fire* tickles our ears. Mom is thrilled with her TRX home gym, holding it close to her chest. I anchor it to the door jam and guide her through some simple squats and rows. She's winded quickly and retreats to the couch with her coffee.

"Oh, I almost forgot," she says, returning to the tree. "You got a card from your father in the mail."

"I don't want it."

She sets the envelope next to me and places a warm hand on my leg. "I'm not saying you have to open it today. Or ever. You can throw it away for all I care."

"Go ahead."

"It's not mine to toss."

"I want nothing to do with him. Why didn't you tell me?"

She takes her hand back to sip her coffee. Eyes on the Christmas tree. "It wasn't my story to tell. Honey, I hate what your father did and it breaks my heart to think about it, but I don't want you resenting him too. I let it eat at me far too long after he left. I don't want that to happen to you, too."

"He cheated on you, Mom."

"Of that I'm well aware."

"And you don't hate him?"

"I did. For a long time. Then I got tired of being angry and hateful inside. It's draining. So, I prayed for him and forgave him in my heart. It was very freeing."

"How could you forgive him?"

"Let's not ruin our Christmas talking about your father. Why don't you save his card for a time when you're ready. He loves you, you know."

I lay my head on her shoulder. "I know he does. I love you, mama bear."

"I love you too. Merry Christmas."

Mom and I spend the rest of Christmas watching our favorite holiday movies with bowls of popcorn. On my drive home, Everly sends me a photo of her with a sparkling new set of golf clubs and a follow up text saying, *It's on Jacoby.*

The only thing better than Christmas is the thought of spending time with Everly and the start of baseball season. Time to ramp things up.

Chapter 15

MONDAY, JANUARY 13, 2020, 9 A.M.

Wendell Pickens Field, Coach's Office

I GET A TEXT FROM Coach Hill, wanting me to stop by his office and discuss the season and my role when my suspension ends. In Fall Ball, I felt I proved enough to earn a starting pitcher role upon my return to play.

"Jacoby, come on in," Coach Hill says. "Close the door behind you."

"How was your break, Coach?"

He shuffles some papers and sets them aside. "A good time with the family. A little golf. And busy getting ready for the season. A lot of tough decisions." He finally looks up at me. "I'll cut right to the chase. With all that went down in Fall Ball aside, we were still happy with the way you threw."

"Thanks, Coach."

"But with the five-game suspension to start the season, we're going in a different direction for our third starter. You'll be coming out of the bullpen to start the year."

Sledgehammer to the gut. Heat fans my face. "Whatever helps the team, Coach. Who won the job over me, if you don't mind me asking?"

"His name's Tyler Waltrip. Goes by Wally. A transfer from Cal State Fullerton. He reached out over the break and was impressive when he threw for us."

A transfer? On a tryout?

"Listen, a lot can happen over the course of a season. Keep working hard and be ready to go after your suspension. You pitch well early and you might find yourself in a different role before you know it."

"Yes, Coach."

"There was something else, but I can't remember right now what that was." He takes off his hat and scratches his salt-and-pepper hair. "I'll remember the second you leave I'm sure."

I turn and depart, leaving his office door open. *Coming out of the bullpen? There goes my season. There goes the draft. There goes a year of rehab and a solid Fall Ball.*

"Johnson." Coach's voice echoes in the hall.

"Something come back to you, Coach?"

"When your suspension is over, you're on pitching chart for the first three innings every game. It'll help you speed up your learning curve on the hitters in this conference." He says it like it's a badge of honor.

"I'm on it, Coach."

In my first class of the semester, Communications and Marketing, the roll sheet has my body marked present but I'm on an emotional bus ride and the bus driver is Bauer's voice.

Jacky boy, tough break kid. Looks like you need an escape? Lucky for you, I've got just the thing, and it's just a few taps away on your phone. You know what I'm talking about. The best release, and it won't cost you a thing!

For the first time, checking out a porn website doesn't sound half bad. Actually, it sounds really good. Bauer's words quickly chain up my wild heart and drag me home after class to meet Jenna, Veronica, Tiffany, and the rest. How I arrive back to Mack's house, I can't remember. Cruise control or something. It doesn't matter. One thing matters. Veronica easing the pain. Keys and phone in hand, I book it for the front door.

"Jacoby." Frank's voice rings out from across the street with his lawn mower. "Left your car door wide open. Everything okay?"

"Fine, Frank. Have a good one." I return and slam it shut. Reroute to the door like a wide receiver with eyes on the end zone and no time on the clock, down by six. I reach for the door with my keys and fumble them along with my phone. Slow motion action unfolds before me as I reach out and bat at my phone to keep the play alive—once, twice, spinning, ricocheting off the front door, twirling out of reach to the ground. My phone hits the concrete face down, which even a cheap phone case can't protect.

No, no, no, no. I turn it over but glass spider webs have already claimed its life, and no amount of CPR is bringing it back.

Still got the computer.

I unlock the door and run down the hall to my room. Anything on my desk is sent flying to the floor. My trembling fingers are ahead of my brain, and I strike out on my first two password attempts before a successful third one grants me computer entry. Bauer's voice is in my ear: *Come on, Jack. The girls are getting restless.*

Icons begin to populate the screen one by one, and I open the web browser. Something from outside my window spooks me.

Was that Frank knocking? No. Keep going. Wait, what do I type? Porn?

A small rotating circle appears on my screen, testing my patience like a junkie seeing his guy roll up an hour late with his fix. Then the phrase *No Internet Connection* flashes on the screen. Are you kidding—

Mack's voice drowns out Bauer's. *One last thing . . . if you want Internet, you'll have to get it yourself . . .*

I slam the screen shut and bury my forehead in my palms, hyperventilating.

When I finally resurface, the chains around my heart are loosened. I expand my lungs to full capacity and deflate them several times, pumping reality back into my system, trying to force out the shame and guilt. Except it's still there. I witness the sobering mess sprawled out around my room—papers, books, and my broken phone. *What'd I almost just do?*

On the floor, sticking out from under the books, lies a square white envelope—the one from my dad.

I open it. It's dated 12/20/19. Three weeks ago.

> *Son,*
>
> *Merry Christmas. I love you more than life itself. I hope you know that. You are the light of my life, and I've been through some dark times of late.*
>
> *I know it's been a while since we spoke. Not a day goes by I wish I could've done things differently. That's the worst part of life. There are no do-overs. Only lessons hopefully learned and wiser decisions made moving forward. I'm still learning that every day.*
>
> *I am nothing but embarrassed and ashamed when I look back at the last time we spoke. I was so caught up in what I wanted and what I felt I deserved that I was blind to the forest I was setting ablaze behind me. I really messed things up, and it's not until recently that I've confronted my actions and taken full responsibility. The fog is clearing. I know this letter alone will not win you back. Nor will it ever repair your mother and me. But I hope it's a start with you and I. Now it's time I be*

honest with you.

I guess it was about the end of your 10th grade season when you were starting to get a lot of attention from scouts. I always reckon time in light of your career for some reason. Your mom and I were becoming distant. She was working a lot and getting her master's at night, and I was starting work in the early morning so I'd never miss your games. Almost without notice, her and I subtly grew apart.

As I read back through this, I realize it may sound like you and your career had something to do with your mother and me splitting. But it's not the case. Our relationship was our responsibility and we didn't, at least I didn't, do my part. As the man in the relationship, it was my privilege to make sure we had our time together and I failed at that. Jacoby, I stopped dating your mom.

I know it sounds hypocritical to be quoting Scripture, but I've learned the best thing to do when I mess up is to run toward God. Not from Him.

1 Corinthians 7:2-5 in the NIV says, "But since sexual immorality is occurring, each man should have sexual relations with his own wife, and each woman with her own husband. The husband should fulfill his marital duty to his wife, and likewise the wife to her husband. The wife does not have authority over her own body but yields it to her husband. In the same way, the husband does not have authority over his own body but yields it to his wife. Do not deprive each other except perhaps by mutual consent and for a time, so that you may devote yourselves to prayer. Then come together again so that Satan will not tempt you because of your lack of self-control."

Jacoby, I knew this stuff . . . but I didn't do it. Know-

ing and doing, I've learned the hard way, are completely different. I didn't listen to God's instructions and suffered the consequences. We were depriving each other, sometimes out of bitterness to punish one another. Sex isn't a weapon or a bargaining piece. It's a blessing from God to grow closer, not a threat to drive discord.

Just so you know, I didn't just decide to jump into bed with another woman one day. It started with us not prioritizing our marriage, which allowed temptation to knock on the door. For me, that temptation was porn.

The letter shakes uncontrollably before I throw the pages down and scoot away. Eyes closed, I take a few breaths before picking the letter back up.

At the time, the advice I got from my male co-workers was that porn wasn't bad or cheating at all. It was normal. They were more surprised that I wasn't already watching it. Soon enough, I was desiring the women on the screen more than your mother. And finally, after a while, the images weren't enough, and that's when I cheated on your mom with another married woman.

A streak of blue ink runs down the page. I wipe it away, forcing myself to read on.

I'll spare you the details, but it brings me to the night we last saw each other. I was still so caught up in the fantasy of it all. Reality hadn't hit. For me at least. Porn makes you numb. Numb to yourself and numb to the people it hurts.

I want you to know this about your mother: She's the most incredible woman in the world, and it took the porn fog finally clearing and my affair fizzling for me to remember that. Pornography traps you and warps reality. It's fantasy. It's not real.

When your mother found out what I was watching, she was humiliated. Despite her heartbreak, she did her best to hold us together, knowing full well she couldn't compete with fantasy. No woman can. Then, when she found out about my affair, she dragged me to Pastor Greg's office, still fighting for us. He gave me an ultimatum that plays on repeat inside me every day: Stop seeing that woman or lose your wife forever. In my selfishness and addiction, I chose to continue my affair. Your mother was crushed.

Jacoby, I realize this is not easy to read. It's even harder to write and hell to experience. The guy you saw last time wasn't the real me. I haven't been the real me for a long time. But I am coming out of the fog and getting the help I need.

Son, don't stumble over the same stumbling blocks that have caused me and those I love so much pain. Porn ruined my life. It started out as something I could control. Something that gave me an escape, made me feel good. Powerful even. Then slowly, and subtly, it gained power over me and consumed me. It promised me everything for free but cost me everything I treasure.

I'm no fool to the goings on of college life, and I'm hoping this reaches you before the temptations of life do. Consider it fatherly advice from someone who doesn't deserve such an incredible son.

I love you. Merry Christmas
Dad

I wipe away a tear before returning the letter to its envelope and rest my mind on my arms. Maybe thirty minutes pass thinking of my dad, my mom, my career, God. And Everly.

I lift my head and walk across the hall to Mack's office for a change of scenery. The lights bring the room to life with all its athletic achievement and glory. The encased Gold Glove glistens in the last bit of sun peeking through the window.

I come across the framed poem next to that 1980 photo of Mack and Suzanne in Yankee Stadium that I'd seen the day of Suzanne's funeral, called *Pray, Don't Find Fault*:

Pray, don't find fault with the man who limps,
Or stumbles along the road
Unless you have worn the shoes he wears
Or struggled beneath his load.
There may be tacks in his shoes that hurt,
Though hidden away from view,
And the burden he bears placed on your back
Might cause you to stumble too.

Don't sneer at the man who's down today,
Unless you have felt the blow that caused his fall,
Or felt the same as only the fallen know,
You may be strong but still the blows that were his,
If dealt to you in the selfsame way at the selfsame
   time,
Might cause you to stagger too.

Don't be too harsh with the man who sins,
Or pelt him with words of stone,
Unless you are sure, yea, doubly sure,
 That you have no sins of your own.
For you know perhaps if the tempter's voice,
Should whisper as soft to you as he did to him
When he went astray,
'Twould cause you to falter too.

—Author Unknown

I unhinge the glass frame and study it in the leather seat across from Mack's desk. I whisper a line, "Don't be too harsh with the man who sins, or pelt him with words of stone, Unless you are sure, yea, doubly sure, That you have no sins of your own."

More tears well up, and the words blur. A few blinks later, I'm face to face with my reflection. A broken kid. I divert my eyes, but Mack and Suzanne continue to stare at me from Old Yankee Stadium. I hear Mack's words: *You never forget the day you get that call. I expect you to buy my a plane ticket when it's your turn.*

I run through the poem once more before hanging it back up. I slowly back my way out of the room, giving Mack's office a once over.

The sun sets on a lonely spot on the wall, still begging to be outfitted with a jersey.

Earn your spot right there, Jacoby. Starting now.

I turn off the lights and pull the doors shut.

Chapter 16

TUESDAY, JANUARY 14, 2020, 7:47 A.M.

Mack's House

"I'M IN," I TELL Mack through the home phone.

"You're in?"

"I'm all in."

"I'm still not following. And why are you calling from the house phone?"

"I broke my phone yesterday. Not on purpose. But whatever you tell me to do, I'm all in. I'm ready to get back on track to get drafted."

"What's going on?"

"I lost the starter spot to a Cal State Fullerton transfer. To be honest, I'd never experienced rejection in baseball. I don't know . . .

I just kind of lost it. Mack, I've never even told you why I got kicked out of my place."

"Some things don't need explaining."

"Well, I need to get it off my chest. I partied with the wrong crowd and slept with my teammate's girlfriend. Almost twice. My teammate! He socked me in the face but he obviously didn't hit me hard enough."

"I might've heard from Frank about a black eye."

"Then yesterday, when I found out some guy took my starting spot after one frickin' tryout, I went berserk. I just wanted to escape. That's part of how I broke my phone. When the rage finally settled, I found a letter from my dad from Christmas. I finally read it."

"What made you open it?"

"I'm not sure. Maybe for a distraction. It definitely wasn't easy to read. I went in your office afterwards to clear my head and came across that poem on your wall."

"*Pray, Don't Find Fault.*"

"Yeah. That's it."

"It's a good one. Humbling."

"Seriously. I read it a few times. It hit me harder than Tim's fist. It made me realize that I'm no better than my dad. I've been bad mouthing and resenting him for what he did, when it was really me and the choices I've been making that I was resenting and ashamed of."

"That's a hard realization."

"Yeah."

"I'm not privy to the contents of your dad's letter, but you're right. Sin is sin in God's eyes. I still remember the day I hung that poem. I placed it there, so I'd read it every day. A sobering reminder to have empathy and be quick to forgive not only others—but ourselves, too. A reminder that we're no better than anyone else."

"Yup. I got that from the poem, too."

"Jacoby, we never know what's going on in the life or heart of another person unless he or she tells us. And even then, we might not get all the details. We're all human. We all need love, and we all need second chances. Or third chances. Or fiftieth chances."

"But I told myself I'd never forgive him."

"Do you still feel that way?"

"After reading that letter . . . and that poem . . . I'm not so sure. But I don't want to think about that right now. I just want to get ready for the season. My focus is getting drafted and putting my jersey up on your wall."

"You realize you're still just a pitch away from being a starter, right?"

Classic Mackism.

"Baseball's a funny game," he continues, "and college ball's even funnier. Injuries, poor grades, shenanigans off the field, inconsistent play—things can change quickly. Do your part in being prepared for your hinge moment."

"What's a hinge moment?"

"It's from Dr. Rob Bell. It's when the door swings open with an opportunity for you to shine. Your job's to be ready for it. My guess is you'll be on Coach Hill's radar right from the start of season."

"Yeah, about that . . . I never told you, but I'm suspended the first five games of the season."

"Then he'll definitely be watching to see how gritty you are when you get back."

"I doubt it. I'll be charting pitches."

"It doesn't matter what role he gives you to do. You think this'll be the last time you ever fight for the mound?"

"No."

"Then you've got two options. Fight or fold."

"I'm fighting."

"Good. Now we need to settle some other things. Like how you're going to go about things with this new teammate of yours. I don't think I need to expound on how bitterness, anger, and resentment are all about to descend on your mental doorstep like a bunch of trick-or-treaters. How much good will it do you to harbor any bitterness toward this guy? Or anger? Or jealousy? Or hate? Tell me when to stop."

"I get it. But—"

"No buts. There's no use feeling sorry for yourself. It'll devour you—first in your thoughts, then in your words, and finally in your performance. Who else will that impact?"

"The team."

"Right. Have you even met this new pitcher yet?"

I pause and take a breath. "No."

"Well, who knows? You might just become best friends. Maybe he can offer some advice on what it's like at the D-1 level. Maybe he's Christian. Maybe he's not and you're just the guy to speak the Word to him to get him born again. Did you ever think of that?"

"No. Sometimes I just can't control how I feel—"

"Of course you can. Who's in control? You or your emotions? We've been over this too many times for you to allow your emotions to get the best of you. The mental game is easy to learn, but it's a whole different ball game to put into practice. Are you going to be a knower or a doer?"

"A doer."

"Then act like it. It's up to you how you'll take ownership of Jacoby, Inc. You're a corporation, you know. A business, with stock that either rises or falls. You need to ask yourself when you're going to stop complaining and start upping your stock, not only to earn playing time but also in contributing to your team. Remember, life's going to happen to you. *That* you can't control. How you respond to what happens to you is completely in your control."

It's the millionth time I've heard him utter those words. But this time they make it through the ear wax. "So, what should I do?"

"What does God's Word say you should do?"

"Come on, Mack."

"Hey, if we're going to do this the right way, God's way, it might benefit you to understand why. Got your Bible handy?"

"I'll grab it."

Moments later, I have the cordless house phone on speaker and I'm opening my Bible at the kitchen counter. "Where are we headed?"

"Colossians 3."

My fingers flip towards the back of my Bible as Mack's pages crackle through the phone. He starts up: "Colossians 3:1-2 in the NIV say, 'Since, then, you have been raised with Christ, set your hearts on things above, where Christ is, seated at the right hand of God. Set your minds on things above, not on earthly things.' Jacoby, where have your sights been?"

"Yeah. On earthly things, I guess."

"Let's see where God instructs us to get our vision in verse 12: 'Therefore, as God's chosen people, holy and dearly loved, clothe your-selves with compassion, kindness, humility, gentleness and patience.'"

Mack pauses while I digest the verses.

"There's your roadmap, Jacoby. It's not the natural reaction to want to be kind to your new teammate. But God's love has nothing to do with your emotional state and everything to do with a decision to love regardless of circumstances. It would also serve as a great example to your teammates. After all, it's your spot you seem to think he took. If *you're* not mad at him, then your teammates have no reason to be, either."

"True. I hate when you make so much sense."

He laughs. "Hey, be mad at God's Word. Not me."

"Nah, I needed to hear it."

"Just remember, when your perspective shrinks to field level, get your eyes back up and remind yourself of what we established together in 2018 for why you want to get drafted. Do you still remember?"

I close my eyes. "I said I wanted to play for God's glory and get drafted so I could have a platform to share about Jesus Christ with the world."

"Well, let's get back to that perspective. You, as a Christian, have the opportunity to be a spokesman for Christ. When people see you . . . they should see Christ. A high calling? Absolutely. But well worth it. You have the ability to take someone from spiritual death to eternal life. *That's* who you are. Baseball is what you do. Instead of bitterness, anger, and jealousy towards this new guy, God's Word says to be compassionate, kind, humble, gentle, and patient. And if God encourages us to do this . . ."

"It must be possible. Yeah, I hear you."

"And hey, coming out of the bullpen and being in charge of the pitching chart may not be your dream jobs, but why not do them with everything you've got? As if Jesus Christ himself asked you to do them? What might happen if you just go through the motions on the pitching chart?"

"I might do the same on the mound."

"Exactly. I think it's great you got assigned the pitching chart. You don't have to love it or love coming out of the bullpen, but you can still choose to invite God into your work. It makes it easier to enjoy every aspect of the craft. That's how you become the best at what you do. And in the end, that's what you're trying to do. Become one of the top pitchers in baseball."

I pause. "It won't be easy for the new guy coming in this late to try and fit in with the team."

"True."

"Maybe I can help him feel at home. Feel part of the team. It might help him pitch better. Thanks, Mack."

An hour later, Mack sends me a text, telling me to be on the lookout for a package of mental game goodies. Time to make nice with the new guy.

Chapter 17

THURSDAY, FEBRUARY 6, 2020, 2:32 P.M.

Wendell Pickens Field Clubhouse

OUR RECORD IS 3-2 when I rejoin the team. I practiced with the guys yesterday and met Tyler Waltrip, but we said nothing more than a few words to each other.

Today, I arrive at the field two-and-a-half hours before game time, and the clubhouse padlock is already unhinged. Tyler is seated and facing his locker in full uniform.

"What you got there?" I ask from my locker, noticing a small laminated square in his hands. He doesn't move.

"Yo, Tyler."

Still nothing. I walk over and he's transfixed on a 10x10-inch mixed-numbers grid similar to ones Mack gave me for mental focus training. Starting at zero, the goal is to find each number as fast as possible in ascending order from 0 to 99 amidst a sea of scattered numbers.

Nothing like breaking in the new guy with a little locker room fun.

I pepper his ear. "You suck at this, Tyler. My grandma woulda finished by now. Seven, 48, 19, 72—you can't find the number, it's not there. Do you have a girlfriend? I hope not because she's fair game if you bring her to the field. You know that, right?"

He's a statue. *Impressive.* I nudge him repeatedly. I run back to my locker and retrieve the ultimate test. I inch my jock strap closer to his face. "Gas mask time."

Still nothing.

Suddenly, the statue comes to life and backhands my cup across the room. "Get that little sunflower seed out of here."

Tyler flashes a big smile.

I point to his concentration grid. "Nice to see someone else working the mental game."

He grabs a handful and offers me a few. "No one around here seems to care much for it."

"Nope. I get crap all the time for all the mental game stuff I do, but it works."

"Yeah, we had Brian Cain come in last semester at Fullerton to introduce the mental game. Game-changer for sure. I've been doing these C-grids before games ever since."

I pick up my jock strap across the room. "I think it took me fifteen minutes the first time I did one of those grids."

"They're not easy. What's your best time?" he asks.

"Like a minute-thirty."

"Same here." He holds up his finished C-grid. "Thanks for the distractions. It's never quiet out there on the mound. My preparation in here shouldn't be either."

I nod and head back to my locker to begin my own mental preparation. A flushing sound rushes from my locker.

"Dude," Tyler says as he approaches me. "What is all that stuff? Your locker looks like Sid's backyard from *Toy Story*."

He's right. Mack's care package of mental game goodies litters my locker. "Where do you want me to start?"

Tyler picks up a palm-sized toilet. "You have got to be kidding." When he lifts the lid, the toilet makes a flushing sound again.

"That's for when I want to flush away the crap that's bothering me in life," I say. "Sometimes I have to flush twice."

He lifts the lid again, playing with it like a kid on his birthday. "I like the metaphor—"

"You're welcome to use it anytime. I bring it with me on the road too. If I have a bad outing, I just flush it so I'm free to become who I need to be next."

He hands me back the toilet and gently swings a beanie baby hanging in my locker by a piece of dental floss around his neck. "What's up with this guy?"

"That's Old Man Bernie. He's my reminder to kill off any old negative thinking patterns that tend to knock me off the mound before the opponent gets the chance."

Next, I show him my taped-up *New Man* poster of motivating quotes and Bible verses that feed me positive verbal ammo. Next to it is a handwritten list. "This is my human highlight reel that I use to remind myself of all my greatest moments. I read the list every day and finish with this quote: 'You've done it before. Do it today.'"

Tyler repeats the quote under his breath.

"Gotta build confidence before you need it," I tell him. I hand him a small red plastic gift, wrapped in a green bow. "Can you guess what this is all about?"

Tyler studies the toy and strokes his stubble. "It's a present . . . oh, I get it. Play in the present moment! That's awesome."

"Yup. The present moment is a gift. It's where action happens. This toy reminds me to be fully present for each pitch I throw."

"And you go through the same routine with all these every day?"

"Every day. A small investment with a huge payoff."

His eyes survey my locker. I continue the tour, explaining how the shiny fishhook represents the lure of getting caught up on little things like poor umpire calls or crappy mound conditions.

"You should open an eBay store with all this stuff."

"Thought about it already." I grin and hand him a foot-long piece of rope. "Notice anything?"

He examines it up and down, then twirls it. "Nope."

"Look closer."

He brings it eye level. "There's a little piece of red floss."

"This end" —I tap the end near the floss—"represents the beginning of my life. And that end, if it could go on forever, represents eternity."

"What about the floss?"

"That represents how brief my baseball career is compared to my overall life."

He laughs and continues to twirl the rope, running his thumb and forefinger the length of it.

"This rope helps me keep baseball in perspective. We've got the tiny width of this floss to play this game and then we have the rest of our lives. And depending on what you believe, some of us have eternity to look forward to. Are you a Christian?"

"I'm thinking about it." Air forces its way from his nostrils as he smiles big.

He hands me back the rope, and I wrap it up like a garden hose. "When I think the world is ending after a bad performance or think I'm the best thing since sliced cheese after pitching great, I come in here and grab this rope and stare at that tiny red floss. Humbles me real quick."

"That's a cool perspective."

"Lately I've realized the things I accomplish in baseball will be forgotten quickly, but what I do for God in sharing about His Son

Jesus Christ will be remembered for eternity. That's the big picture goal for me. I've known it for a while. Now I believe it."

"I've never met someone so into the God stuff. Not a bad thing. Just rare."

"I don't flaunt my beliefs, but I don't shy away from them anymore, if someone asks. Honestly though, my faith is my best mental weapon. I'd be happy to open the Bible with you when you're interested."

"Maybe," he says, as his cleats head for the clubhouse door. "Thanks for showing me your stash. I might be borrowing some of your ideas."

"If anything's missing, I know who to come after. Glad to have someone else around here who appreciates the mental game. And just so you know, I'm pulling for you out there today."

"I appreciate that."

Soon after, the clubhouse is buzzing with chatter. On the couch, I begin my breathing exercises. In through the nose, out through the mouth. Smooth, relaxed, deep breaths filling my lungs to capacity, before releasing. Then, in my mind gym, I throw fastballs with whiffle ball-like movement to the glove.

Rinse, repeat, compete.

Game time.

7:14 P.M.
Wendell Pickens Field

Tied 1-1 going into the 7th, Tyler is approaching 100 pitches. With our best reliever, Gleyber Rodriguez, ready in the bullpen, and Tyler having walked the first batter, Coach Hill heads to the mound to make the change. Wally receives high fives from all of us in the dugout.

On Rodriguez's first pitch, we have a tailor-made double play hit to our third basemen who fields the grounder but airmails the second baseman by five feet. Coach Hill is pacing the dugout, staring down our third basemen. Runners on the corners, still no one out.

The next batter walks on a borderline 3-2 fastball to load the bases. Coach Jenkins canes his way to the mound to calm Rodriguez but whatever was discussed didn't seem to work as the very next pitch is launched like a rocket over the left field scoreboard. Unfortunately, all of Tyler's hard work sails out of the ballpark with it. The score, 5-1 Hornets.

"Johnson, get loose," Coach Hill hollers down the dugout. *Awesome. Cleaning up the trash. At least I'm back on the mound.*

By the time I enter the game, we've given up another run and have baserunners on first and third, one out, score 6-1. The home crowd has flatlined. I toe the rubber from the stretch. From his previous at-bats, this guy likes to pull the ball. The catcher signals for a two-seam in. I shake him off and agree on a change-up low and away. I come to a set position, pausing for a deep breath. Exhale . . . and deliver.

"Good pitch, Jacky boy," Coach Jenkins shouts from the dugout. "Just like that now."

A blip on the crowd pulse fights to regain life. *Deep breath.* Catcher flashes the same sign. Bold, but I like it.

"Strike two," the umpire calls.

The catcher calls for the curve. *No. Batter's looking for it.* Fastball inside. I come set, check the runners, and deliver. A full swing but a jam shot back to me. I field and fire to second base. Tim receives the ball chest high and slings it to first for the double play. The fans erupt. Three pitches. Out of the jam. Invigorating fist bumps fill the dugout, including Coach Hill. "You're going back out there."

"Yes, Coach."

We put up a two-spot in the bottom of the 7th, and I follow it up with a quick 1-2-3 top of the 8th to get us back on offense. The score is 6-3, bottom of the 8th.

"Let's go, boys!" Coach Jenkins yells, the Little Leaguer in him coming to life. "You puttin' a lil' spook in dat dugout over there."

We scrape together a couple of baserunners with two outs with our No. 3 hitter stepping into the batter's box. Their pitcher misses his spot for a 400-foot mistake.

"See ya, ball!" I shout, as we all lean over the railing to watch the ball sail over the left-center fence.

Suddenly, we have ourselves a ballgame, tied 6-6, heading into the 9th. Coach says nothing, and with no bullpen activity, I make my way to the mound chest out and chin up. The pop of the catcher's mitt during warm-ups lets me know I have plenty in the tank. The mound feels like it's 20 feet away from home plate. The best feeling for any pitcher. With the first two hitters, I'm on autopilot, getting my sign and throwing to the mitt like a game of catch with ghost batters, before finally surrendering a walk. *Can't have two out walks.*

Sweat drips from my bill. *New moment, Jacoby. Focus on the next guy.* I pick up the rosin bag and cause a dust cloud around the mound as I dry myself from hand to forearm.

Over the PA system, the announcer echoes, "Now pinch hitting, *hitting, hitting* . . . for the Hornets, *Hornets, Hornets* . . . Shawn, *Shawn, Shawn,* Bauer, *Bauer, Bauer.*"

The boos from the crowd let me know I'm not hearing things. Bauer is staring me down with a smug look. I'd totally forgotten he was on their team. I'd forgotten about our bet.

I brush him back with a first-pitch fastball, nearly hitting him in the ribs. That was to send a message. On my second delivery, same thing, but it wasn't on purpose, never wanting to fall behind in the count. My cleats pierce the turf just behind the mound. I remove my hat, dry my forehead with my forearm, pick up the rosin bag again, and take a deep breath. *One pitch at a time.*

We're not getting drunk at the Ducks game.

The next pitch I snap off a nasty curve that starts eye level, causing him to bail out of the batter's box to the amusement of the crowd.

"Stee-rike."

Whether Bauer is staring me down or laughing it off, I could care less. The catcher's mitt is begging for the same pitch. I gather myself, check the runner, and snap it off.

This time my curve hangs more lifeless than my stocking the day after Christmas.

Ping . . .

The loneliest sound in the world hushes the crowd. I know it already and don't even turn. It's a 7-6 ball game. As Bauer rounds the bases, I signal to the umpire to give me another ball.

"Blue," I shout, getting his attention with my glove out. "Ball."

Before I can retreat to the mound, the umpire calls "Time."

No. No. No. Coach Hill is making his way toward me. Just like that, my night is over. I forfeit the ball to Coach Hill. Even though that pitch probably lost the game, his butt slap lets me know I've moved up a notch on his bullpen belt. Unfortunately, we fail to score in the bottom of the ninth and lose.

Back in the clubhouse, I'm changing out of my uniform when water rushes. I finish pulling off my jersey, and Tyler is playing with my mini-toilet. He flushes it again before handing it to me. "One pitch. Flush it. Don't let it overshadow how good you were tonight."

"Sorry I couldn't salvage all your hard work," I tell him.

"That's pitching, man. That's baseball."

"True."

"I'll let you get to your toys."

I flush the toilet, close my eyes, and let the sound wash over my performance. Tyler's right. One bad pitch and Bauer made me pay. That's baseball.

At my car, there's a visitor waiting for me: Shawn Bauer. He's sporting his *I-told-you-so grin.* "I prefer second deck, center ice."

"Were you sitting on that curve?"

"Of course I was. Who caught you all fall?"

I hadn't thought of that. "Well, you sure guessed right on that pitch."

"I know, right? Oh, and I prefer 805 Beer. Ice cold."

"I'll see you next week," I say, pushing him off my car.

"Can't wait."

On my drive home, all I want to hear is Everly's voice. When she picks up, she sounds exhausted.

"Hey there, pretty lady. Was just thinking about you."

"I like that. Sorry I wasn't there tonight. My English professor thinks the world revolves around her. How are you?"

"We lost."

"Did you pitch?"

"I did."

"You don't sound too happy."

"It was good and bad."

"You say every performance is good and bad."

"I mean I've got good news and bad news. The good news is I pitched really well overall and think I earned more opportunities moving forward. The bad news is Bauer hit a home run off me that cost us the game."

"Didn't you two have a—"

"Yes. And I lost."

"So . . ."

"I'm taking him to the Ducks game next week."

"Why do I feel like there's more to the story?"

Silence. "Part of the bet was that we'd drink before the game. I said yes to it because I thought it was a one-in a million chance."

More silence. "Where are you?"

"On the freeway."

"I need a study break. Come over. I'll cook something."

Oh boy. "I think I'll just pick something up on the way home. What about tomorrow—"

"Jacoby, I want to talk about this tonight."

"I'll see you in a few."

Chapter 18

THURSDAY, FEBRUARY 6, 2020, 9:46 P.M.

OUTSIDE EVERLY'S APARTMENT, I dabble on my phone for 15 minutes in my car. When I knock, she unlocks the door but barely opens it. I nudge the door open. Her blonde bun, black yoga pants, and orange practice shirt are walking back to the kitchen.

"Smells good," I yell over the stove fan.

"Chicken, rice, and salad."

Still no eye contact.

"How's the homework coming?"

"Almost done."

The stove fan fills the silence.

"I know you're not thrilled about me going with Bauer to that hockey game."

"How'd you guess?"

"You haven't looked at me yet."

She looks up. "If you want to go to the game with him, go to the game. But I'm not a fan of you drinking with him before the game."

"I don't even want to go with him at all. But I gave him my word."

"So what? I'm all for integrity, but for this? Come on. What's more important? A stupid bet or your relationship with God? Or your baseball career? Or me?"

"What does this have to do with God?"

"A lot. I don't know everything about what happened this fall, but from what you've told me it didn't sound like you and God were exactly on fire. And it all seemed to stem from you spending time with Bauer, your drinking buddy."

I grab two place settings for the table. "I'm past all that, Ev. It's just this one time."

"You don't know that. You mix alcohol and Bauer and you're asking for trouble, especially in public. You're not even 21."

I fiddle with a napkin. *Forks go on the left*? "I get what you're saying. But it'll be fine."

Her tone softens as she takes my face in her hands, "Listen, I care about you. You know that. Let's enjoy dinner, and afterward I'd like to share some Scriptures with you. That way, if you want to argue with someone, you can argue with God. Okay?" She kisses me on the forehead.

We sit down to herb-crusted chicken, Spanish rice, and a salad with home-made dressing topped with sliced strawberries. As Everly prays for the meal, my choo-choo train alert from my phone goes off in my pocket, but I ignore the incoming text.

After dinner, we clear our plates and clean the kitchen before settling into the living room. I can't help but smile and shake my head. "I hope you're not going to use the Bible against me."

"Oh, I'm not," she says, propping a pillow up on her lap as a table.

"I'm very much using it *for* you."

She lays her NIV Bible on the pillow and flips the pages. "How much do you love winning?"

"That's random."

"How much?"

"Of course I love winning."

"More than anything?"

"Sure."

"What about losing? How much do you hate losing?"

"Just as much."

"Good. A great player has to love winning *and* hate losing. Now, how much do you love God?"

"Ev, where are you going with this?"

"Just humor me."

"Of course I love God."

"And how much do you hate evil?"

"As much as possible."

"See? That's where you're wrong."

"How so?"

"Jacoby, if you love God, you have to love what He loves and hate what He hates. Listen to Proverbs 8:13: 'To fear the Lord is to hate evil; I hate pride and arrogance, evil behavior and perverse speech.' God hates evil, and I'm not so sure you do. You're flirting with it if you go drinking with Bauer before that game."

"I'm just going to have one beer. It's part of the bet."

"I'm not preaching at you, babe. I'm trying to sharpen you. That's my privilege as your sister in Christ." She kisses my cheek and whispers in my ear, "Who happens to like you. A lot."

"I'm listening."

She flips to another passage. "Proverbs 13:20 says, 'Walk with the wise and become wise, for a companion of fools suffers harm.' Who we spend time with matters. People will either push you toward God or pull you away from Him. I just don't see how Bauer pushing a beer can into your hands is going to bring you closer to God."

How can I be mad at logic? "I get it. But I'm not always going to be surrounded by Christians."

She cups her hands under my chin, making sure I'm trained on her. "But you don't have to go looking for the wrong crowd. Isn't that what you're doing?"

"You should be a lawyer."

"Jacoby, I'm serious," she's says, holding back a laugh. "I'm not trying to ruin your fun. I'm just saying that's not the kind of fun worth having." She flips toward the back of her Bible. "Ephesians 5:18 says, 'Do not get drunk on wine, which leads to debauchery. Instead, be filled with the Spirit.' Bauer drinks to get drunk and who knows what he's liable to do. That's not the kind of spirit you want to be filled with."

Again, she has a point.

"There's one more in Proverbs 24 I want to show you," she says. "In verses 1 and 2 it says, 'Do not envy the wicked, do not desire their company; for their hearts plot violence, and their lips talk about making trouble."

"But Bauer isn't a wicked dude. He just needs a friend."

"Jacoby, when God mentions wickedness and evil, He's not talking about some black cloud lurking in the shadows. No one would envy that. But we might envy someone who's successful, rich, witty, or talented. My mentor says it's like a fish hook with shiny bait. The offer is alluring until you bite down and it takes your life. That's the devil's game plan, and he's not afraid to use the people around us to execute it. You've already experienced it enough times with Bauer to know better. Can't you see what you're about to walk back into?"

I close my eyes, momentarily. Her argument's air tight. "I hear you. And I'm thankful that you care enough about me to talk it out."

"Then break it off. Call or text him. Buy tickets for him and a buddy but don't go to that game."

"I'll think about it."

"Jacoby . . ."

"I said I'll think about it. I really do appreciate the wisdom, yoda."

Her lips try hard not to bend. "I'm serious."

"Oh, I'm dead serious too." I wrap her in my arms and kiss her forehead. "I need to go pack."

She walks me to the door, "I'm praying for God to give you wisdom. Be safe and smart on your road trip. I know how those can go."

"Goodnight, pretty lady. Dinner's on me next time."

At my car, I check my missed text message from dinner.

Bauer: What do you mean you're not going? That wasn't the deal. Whatever bro

Little did Everly know, I'd already bought Bauer two tickets and Venmo'd him beer money. But I had to come face the music. I needed to make sure I'm investing in a woman who's going to call me out on my crap. Everly's boldness, care, and willingness to confront me with the Word only solidifies my heart further. I love this girl.

Now, on to a little baseball in Bakersfield.

Chapter 19

FRIDAY FEBRUARY 7, 2020, 7:28 A.M.

"JOHNSON, GET OVER HERE," Coach Hill calls as we're boarding the bus for the Bakersfield tournament.

Pillow and duffel in hand, I hustle over to him. "Yes, Coach?"

"How do you think you pitched last night?"

Bauer's home run explodes on mental replay. "Overall, pretty good. Room for improvement, of course."

"I agree." An awkward smirk peeks across his face. "How would you like to close for us?"

"What about Rodriguez?"

"Do you see him here?"

Guys are loading up on the bus. He's not one of them.

"I got a call from the academic counselor," Coach says. "He's ineligible due to his fall grades. Opens the door for someone to step in. Despite your lack of innings, I like what you showed us last night."

Mack's hinge moment. "Thank you, Coach. Happy to help the team however you see fit."

"Good. The closer's job is yours to lose."

On the bus, everyone's nestled up with their pillows and earbuds. "Listen up," Coach Hill hollers. "Sophomores, you know the road trip rules. Listen anyways. Freshman, pay attention. Road trips are a privilege. Not a right. You get a $20 per diem for food so use it for food. Understood?"

"Yes, Coach," we call back in tired voices.

"Coach Jenkins will pass out meal money and roommate assignments when we exit the bus. Curfew is 11 p.m. unless we're still at the field. What time is curfew?"

"11 p.m."

"There will be no alcohol, period. No drugs, period. No girls in the rooms, period. Is that clear?"

"Yes, Coach."

"That's about it for the rules. Coach Jenkins, am I missing anything?"

"I think dat 'bout covers it. Them boys too dang ugly to git a girl back to their room, anyway."

Laughter erupts. Even Coach Hill cracks a semblance of a smile. "Final thing, gentlemen. You'll notice Gleyber Rodriguez didn't make the trip. Unfortunately, he slacked off in the fall and didn't make grades, and it caught up to him. I harp on you all fall about your grades. Your schoolwork affects you, your future, and this team. But it also opens an opportunity for other guys to step up. Jacoby Johnson will be closing games from here on out until he shows me otherwise. Let's go take care of business in Bakersfield."

I receive a few pats on the shoulder before we try to doze off for a couple hours.

The long bus ride through Los Angeles and over the Grapevine doesn't seem to have any effect on us as we jump out to an early 3-0 lead in the top of the first.

By the end of the 7th, we're up 6-4 and I begin to loosen my limbs in anticipation of the ninth inning. *It's still baseball. Still one pitch at a time. Don't add unnecessary pressure. Bask in the pleasure.*

The top of the 8th rolls along, and I begin throwing lightly in the pen. The ball comes out smooth and effortlessly, popping the catcher's mitt. We don't score in either the top of the eighth or ninth, leaving the score 6-4 when I jog to the game mound to close it out. *Feel the ground. Each step, each stride. Smell the grass, slow the moment. Be here now.*

My warm-up tosses feel as good as they did in the bullpen and show late action down in the zone. After my last toss, I duck the oncoming throw to Tim at the second base bag and walk behind the mound. *Nice deep breaths, big guy. It's your turn. Best pitcher in baseball. Best pitcher in baseball. Me and you, God.*

"Here we go, Jacky Boy," Coach Jenkins shouts.

A lefty steps to the plate who had a base hit early in the game—a six hole shot. Catcher calls for fastball away. I shake him off. Fastball in? Yes. Into the windup. Deliver.

"Stee-rike."

"Just like that," Tim shouts from shortstop.

The catcher puts down three fingers for a change-up. Shake. Fastball away? Shake. Fastball in? Nod. Into the windup and deliver. *Ping.* He smashes it deep down the right field line with the right fielder giving chase—I hold my breath. Just foul.

New moment. The catcher calls for a change-up away. Shake. Fastball up? Yup. Now we're on the same page. Deep breath. Windup and deliver. His barrel misses by a full inch. Strike three swinging.

One down.

"Great job, Jacky," Tim calls out from short while the ball zooms around the infield like a pinball ball before returning with a heavy thud to my glove. *Win this next pitch. Be here.*

The rest of the inning is a locked-in effortless flow with the next batter popping up a 2-1 curveball and the third batter swinging at a change-up in the dirt for strike three. Game over. Save number one and a win to start the tournament.

Coach doesn't say much after the game other than "Good job." He reminds us of our 11 p.m. curfew and our doubleheader starting tomorrow morning. He tells me I likely won't pitch tomorrow since I'd thrown almost three innings yesterday and an inning today, but if needed, I'd pitch Sunday. We're throwing our gear on the bus when Coach Jenkins lets me know there's someone standing near the back of the bus wanting to talk. It's the Angels scout, Branch Calderone, in khaki pants and a red polo.

"You looked great out there today, Jacoby." We shake hands.

"Thank you. Feels good to be back on the mound."

"They've got you coming out of the bullpen now?"

"For now at least. Coach Hill's idea."

"Well, you might want to thank him. You hit 96 mph today. That's the fastest I've ever seen you throw. Showed good command of your off speed, too."

"I hit 96?" I laugh. I have to. I'd never thrown faster than 94 for a gun before.

"I checked with two other scouts. They got the same radar reading I did. Who knows? You just might drive up your draft stock as a back-end reliever or an opener now that baseball is trending in that direction. We've got our eyes on you."

I board the bus, and everyone's looking at me like I just got the phone number of the hottest girl in school. I feel like I did, too. When Branch is far enough away from the bus, they erupt in excitement for me.

After showering at the hotel, a few of us head out for a burger when the topic of women circles the group. Most of the chatter is about who is sleeping with whom and how good everyone thinks they are in bed. I do my best to keep silent and eat fast, but Tim calls me out.

"I hear you're dating Everly? Volleyball chick, right?"

"Yeah."

"How's she in the sack?"

"We don't" —I wipe my mouth—"We aren't doing that stuff."

"Why not?"

"We're just deciding not to for now."

"So you hooked up with Fallon but you're not hooking up with Everly?"

We'd never personally discussed what happened with Fallon. "It's not like that."

"You and your religious crap. Kind of a hypocrite, don't you think?"

"I never said I was perfect. I'm just trying to do things the right way this time."

"And not having sex is the right way?" Everyone laughs.

"Just trying to do what the Bible says is what I meant. Didn't turn out so hot when I tried the other way with Fallon, did it?"

Tim's cheeks flush.

Another teammate chimes in, "If you're not having sex on the regular why even have a girlfriend?"

"There's more to a girlfriend than sex," Tyler chimes in.

"There is?" Tim asks, causing enough laughter to draw attention to our table.

Tim turns to me. "We're just messing with you, Jack. Keep throwing like you're throwing and we all might stop having sex."

I paint on a smile as everyone enjoys a good laugh at my expense—everyone except Tyler. Either he's on my side because he's rooming with me or he doesn't find it funny either. After we finish our burgers, we get up to leave and Tim turns to me and Tyler. "A couple of us are grabbing some beer from the store. You guys in?"

"I'm good," Tyler says, heading for the door.

"What about you, Jacky boy? A beer won't kill you. You're just sitting on the bench tomorrow anyways."

Could be my chance to repair things with Tim. "What's your room number?"

"Come to 204 in about thirty minutes."

"I might stop by just to say hi."

They head toward the gas station, and I catch up to Tyler at the crosswalk. He waits for me to get close before saying, "You know you don't have to meet up with them?"

"I know."

"Then why are you risking everything? You heard Coach on the bus."

"I'd have one beer max. I've been trying to figure a way to repair things with Tim. This might be my chance."

"With those guys it's never just one beer."

"You barely know them."

"I don't have to know them personally. I know the type. I saw it at Fullerton all the time. How do you think I ended up here?"

The crosswalk sign lights up. "I heard rumors . . . but I wasn't going to ask."

"Now you know for sure. I got busted for drinking on a roadtrip and got kicked out of the baseball program. I see the road you're on, bro. It's the same one I've already been down."

We get to the hotel, and he stops just short of the elevator. "In a few months, I'm going to flip on ESPN and likely see my old team-mates in Omaha playing for the College World Series. I have to live with that. But at least I've learned from my mistake."

Ding.

"You coming up?" he asks.

"I'm gonna hang in the lobby for a bit and call my girlfriend."

He steps inside. "I'm not stopping you. Just offering some advice that cost me everything but'll cost you nothing, if you listen."

I nod. "Thanks, Wally. I'll be up in a bit."

The elevator doors close behind him.

9:17 P.M.

The lobby is empty except for the receptionist answering phones and a few elevator passengers traveling to and from their rooms. I find a comfortable couch and call Everly. No answer. Fifteen minutes later, Coach Jenkins hobbles passed me and reminds me about curfew. "Might be nice to go stick them feet in the jacuzzi. Something you might like out there."

"What's out there?"

"Gonna have to see for yourself." He flashes his gold smile as he canes his way down the hall. Through the window, three teammates are hanging out in the jacuzzi with some girls. Jimmy, our right fielder, spots me and vigorously waves me to join them.

"Dude," he says over the bubble jets, "did you check Twitter?"

"I haven't been on social media in a month."

"Someone posted you hitting 96 today, and it's blowing up." He hands me his phone. There are 13,000 likes and counting. "Everyone's talking about it. Oh, sorry. Jacoby, this is Jessica, Rachel, and . . . sorry what's your—"

"Megan," she says.

"Yes. Megan. Ladies, this is Jacoby. He's going to be a millionaire in a few months."

"Hi," I say, handing Jimmy back his phone.

"There's room for one more," Jessica says, in a red bikini that doesn't cover much.

"Next time, perhaps."

Jessica never takes her eyes off me.

"You ladies are in good hands. Boys, don't forget, 11 p.m. curfew. I'll see you in the morning."

"You're loss, bro." Jimmy's not too mad I'm leaving.

I sit back down in the lobby and try to call Everly. Voicemail again.

"Hey, you." I turn and Jessica is at my side wrapped in a towel, hair dripping down onto my shoulder. "Are you waiting for someone?"

"Just making a call."

"You want to play some cards?"

"In the lobby? In your bathing suit?"

"No, silly." She points down the hallway. "In my room."

"Oh. I, uh, have a girlfriend. Jimmy's single, though."

"Yeah, he told me. About 30 times." She rolls her eyes. "Come play cards with me. I'll teach you a cool game."

"I have curfew in a bit."

"You told them eleven. That's plenty of time."

"What's the card game?"

She reaches for my hand. "You'll just have to wait and see."

I peek back at the jacuzzi. The guys are occupied with Rachel and what's her name. "One game."

We walk down the hallway, and I close her room door behind us. On her way to the mini fridge, she drops her towel, revealing her red bikini bottoms, cut almost like a thong. She bends over to open the fridge, pulls out a handle of vodka, and pours a couple shots into mini Solo cups. "Have you played *Never Have I Ever*?"

"I've watched people play."

"It's okay. You can stare."

"I, umm, sorry."

"I don't mind." She sets a vodka shot down for me on the desk and rubs the seat for me to sit across from her. "What was that Twitter thing all about?"

"Nothing much."

"Those 13,000 likes don't sound like *nothing much*. Are you a celebrity or something?"

"Just a junior college baseball player."

"But you're going pro?"

"That's the goal."

She lifts her shot glass and leans her chest towards me. "Cheers. To pro ball."

I lift mine. She takes her shot without flinching. "What's wrong?"

"You know what? I, um, this is something I want to celebrate with my girlfriend. I'm sorry I wasted your time." I hand her the shot glass. "Have mine."

When her door closes behind me, I exit out of the lobby doors to stand in the brisk February air to clear my head. *What were you thinking?*

Fifteen minutes later, I'm strolling along the downtown main street when Everly's face pops up on my phone. "Hey, Ev."

"Hey, babe. Sorry I missed your calls. Was having dinner with my parents. How are you? Did you throw today?"

"I did. Really well. Someone posted a video of me throwing 96 mph."

"That's like really fast, isn't it?"

I laugh. "You could say that. I also talked to a high-level scout after the game, too."

"How exciting! I'm so proud of you. Hold on, I'm getting a text."

Thirty seconds go by without response.

"Ev, you still there?" *Choo Choo!*. My screen lights up. It's a video text from Everly even though we're still on the phone. I tap the play button. It's a video of me following Jessica's red bikini into her hotel room.

"You want to explain that?"

I'm done. "Ev, I was in the lobby calling you, and my teammate showed me that Twitter post by the spa where they were hanging with some girls. I left and tried to call you again, but there was no answer."

"So it's my fault you followed some girl into her room?"

"No, hear me out. I was in the lobby and she came by and asked if

I wanted to play cards. I had no intention of doing anything. I swear. And just listening to what's coming out of my mouth right now, I have no excuse. It was stupid. I left her room almost immediately."

Silence.

"Ev . . . I'm sorry. I got caught up in the moment. It won't happen again. Ever. You are what I want. You know that."

"How am I supposed to react, Jacoby? We've been seeing each other for two months. Are we just some fling until you go pro and some red bikini bimbo invites you into her room?"

"Not even close. Being in that room with her, I just thought of you and I was sick to my stomach. I left immediately, Ev. I swear. You've got every right to leave me."

"Is that what you want?"

"Not at all."

"Well, this isn't how you treat someone you care about. You had my trust."

Silence is my only companion. My fingers rake my scalp, front to back. "Ev, I wish I could erase the last half hour. I know how important trust is to you, and I promise to do whatever it takes to earn it back. Please, Ev. I had a momentary lapse in judgement. My ego got the best of me. Nothing happened. I swear."

"What were you hoping for when she invited you in?"

"I don't know. Honestly, I don't."

More silence.

"I need some time to think and pray about this. I've been burned bad before, and it just happened all over again."

"Ev, I'm sorry. Truly sorry. I feel sick to my stomach."

"So do I. I just don't know if this is going to work. I'll reach out when I'm ready to talk. I hope you play well the rest of your trip. Goodnight."

"Ev—"

Click.

I stay outside a while longer, walking around aimlessly, enduring the cold as self-inflicted punishment. Out loud I pray, "Heavenly Father, I messed up. Again. You know it. I know it. I'm sorry. Please forgive me for being an idiot. I've got an incredible girl who for some reason likes me, well, liked me, whose heart I just shattered.

"I don't know why I did what I did but I shouldn't have done it. I guess I'm still learning that whole knowing verses doing thing. No excuse, I know. I pray for Everly. That You would mend her heart and give her the wisdom she needs. I love You. Please help me get some sleep. In Christ's name I pray. Amen.

"P.S. I pray for Wally to get some good rest, too. He's starting tomorrow. But You know that. I also pray for another open door to speak the Word to him. Goodnight."

A text comes through from Tim. *How was little red riding hood?*

I don't text back. I want to kill him.

My phone shines a bright 11:07 p.m.. *Oh, crap.* I sprint back to the hotel, then up the stairwell and slowly crack the second floor door. No one. Two doors away from my room, Coach Jenkins turns the corner and spots me. "Who dat? Jacky boy? That you? Stay right there—" he hobbles toward me.

Be cool. Be cool.

"You know what time it is, son?"

"Yes, Coach."

"Then what you doin' out your room?"

A door opens behind Coach Jenkins and Wally emerges from our room with an ice bucket. "Evening, Coach."

"Waltrip, what you boys doing out past curfew?"

"Getting some ice for our arms. Hard to find the machine around here. Thought we'd find it faster if we split up."

"Sounds like some scary movie type stuff. You shoulda iced hours ago. Not gonna do you no good now. That elbow hurtin' you, Jacky boy?"

"Just a precaution, Coach," Tyler says.

"Let the man speak for hisself."

"Just a precaution," I echo.

"Alright then, you boys let me know if them arms start hurtin' for real. Beginning of the season, and y'all already fragile."

"We're good, Coach," I say. "Goodnight."

We're almost in our room when Coach Jenkins calls out, "You know, ice works better when it's actually in da bucket." With a sly grin, he canes his way down the hall.

"Thank you, Coach," I say. "Goodnight again."

I hit the bed with full force, heart still racing. "Thanks, Wally. I owe you big time."

"Get some rest."

I doubt that will happen.

I dodged a bullet with Coach Jenkins. I can only pray Everly will be as forgiving.

Chapter 20

SUNDAY, FEBRUARY 16, 6:56 P.M.

Campus Ministry Meeting

VALENTINE'S DAY CAME AND went without a word from Everly. I had planned to skip the next G2G meeting after the Bakersfield fiasco, but I had asked Tyler during the trip if he was interested in going with me. To my surprise, he said yes, so there was no backing out.

The meeting is just starting when we walk in. Everly is at the front of the room facing a full house of bodies three rows deep. She's wearing a festive pink and purple romper with hearts on it and her blonde hair is straightened. She's never looked more beautiful. *I'm an idiot.*

"Thank you all for coming tonight," she begins as the crowd quiets and settles in. "We have a ton of ground to cover, and as always, I'm excited to be delving into the Scriptures with you all. Let's pray and get started. Heavenly Father, thank you for being accessible and giving us Your listening ear at all hours of the day. Of all Your great creations, You see us as Your greatest masterpiece. Even if we don't feel like it at times . . ."

A few muffled chuckles.

". . . I pray for this evening, for every person in this room. I pray for hearts to be settled and ears to be ready to receive all the love, comfort, and encouragement You have for us as we look at Your Mighty Scriptures. In Jesus' name we pray. Amen."

"Amen."

"I think tonight's topic of performing with God's love is fitting since Valentine's Day just passed. I promise I did not plan it that way. For those of you who have been with us, bear with me as I provide our newcomers with a brief recap of what we've studied this year. I'm sure we all could use a little refresher."

She gathers her notes. "This year our focus has been the renewing of the mind. Our theme verse is Romans 12:2. You don't have to turn there. I'll read it from my notes. It says, 'Do not conform to the pattern of this world, but be transformed by the renewing of your mind. Then you will be able to test and approve what God's will is— his good, pleasing and perfect will.'

"Our goal this year has been to learn how to become transformed by God's Word rather than be conformed to this world. We learned that the first step in renewing the mind is to study the Scriptures. We have to get God's Word rooted in our minds to the point that His perfect words and thoughts become ours. That's the foundation to renewing the mind.

"Then, as we continue to study and grow in God's Word, step two is to control our thinking to recognize who we are in Christ. The world is happy to tell us who we are or who we should become, but it's only from the truth of God's Word that we learn we are God's kids *now* and don't have to succumb to the world's opinions of us.

"We are to be rooted in our identity in Christ and remind ourselves daily that we are incredibly valuable to God with the ability to share about Jesus Christ with others and literally take them from death to eternal life in a single conversation. That's valuable, huh? We're God's first-round draft picks. Better believe it."

She steals a peek at me and winks. *My heart leaps. Dang, I love her.*

"Just like in sport, once we've learned how to do something, what's the next step?"

"Practice," several regulars speak up.

"Right. Step three then is practicing the presence of God in our lives, which we covered last month for those who couldn't make it. We do this by walking and talking with Him throughout our day, bringing our needs and prayer requests to Him. The more we get to know our God from reading about Him in His Word, the more confidence we gain in going to Him for help. Prayer is an incredible alternative to anxiety, fear, or worry. How many of our problems does God want us to cast on Him?"

"All of them," many reply.

"He hears us and is able and willing to provide for us as His kids when we pray according to His will. He says He'll never ever leave us. How comforting, right?"

Head nods. *At least God didn't let her down.*

"Those are some of the benefits we enjoy as we practice God's presence on a moment-by-moment basis. So to recap: Step one is reading God's Word. Step two: recognizing your Christian identity. Step three: take advantage of that relationship by practicing God's presence. And once we've practiced, what's the only thing left to do?"

"Perform," several more say.

"Performance starts in the mind and comes out in our words and actions. So step four is performing with God's love. Without love—God's kind of love I should say—the three previous steps are worthless. The opening verses of 1 Corinthians 13 say that whatever we do, if it's not done with the love of God, it's like sounding brass or a tinkling cymbal. Basically, we're just making a lot of noise."

A few more chuckles filter around the room.

"Honestly, though, just like in sport where it's not about the knowing but about the doing, God would rather us know one single verse and *do* it with love than know the entire Bible cover to cover and not perform a single word of it. I've been blessed and also confronted quite a bit this past week in studying God's love."

I study my Bible cover. *Is she talking about me?*

"It's unlike any other love. I'm about to give you a little geeky Greek, but I think it'll be helpful. As far as I know, there are three kinds of love discussed in the Bible. There's *eros* love, which is the Greek word for romantic love, where you do things out of emotional compulsion rather than by your will. This love comes and goes throughout a relationship. Then there's *phileo* love, where we get the English word Philadelphia, meaning brotherly love, where I do something for you because you did something for me. Following me so far?"

Heads nod.

"Then there's this type called *agape* love. It's a spiritual love from God. It has nothing to do with strong feelings or returning a favor. It's the most mature kind of love because it takes a decision of the mind. It's an all-out devoted love that puts others first despite feelings."

Everly pauses to let her words sink in before continuing.

"There's a verse that probably all of us have heard that demonstrates this agape love really well. Let's flip to John 3:16."

When the rustling pages die down, she begins. "John 3:16 in the NIV says, 'For God so loved the world that he gave his one and only Son, that whoever believes in him shall not perish but have eternal life.' Could you imagine giving up your son? I couldn't. But God did that for us, so that He could have a big ol' family. What else do you guys see with this type of love?"

After a few moments, Rebecca, the softball player, raises her hand. "God's love—how did you say it? Ah-gape?"

"Almost. Ah-gah-pay."

"Agape love seems to be about giving. It says, God so loved . . . that He gave . . ."

"Exactly. Did we deserve God giving us His son?" Everly asks.

A few unconfident heads sway side to side.

"So, we learn here that God's love is not only a decision of the mind, but it's also about giving, even if the recipient doesn't necessarily deserve it. God took the lead in showing His love toward us when we least deserved it. Can you imagine doing that for someone when they don't necessarily deserve it?

"God's love isn't selfish or self-seeking. God so loved the people of this world that He chose to give His only Son on our behalf so that we might benefit from a relationship with Him and spend eternity with Him. Isn't that cool?"

Head nods with smiles.

"Now let's flip a few chapters forward to John, Chapter 13 where we'll see Jesus demonstrate this kind of love toward his disciples during the Last Supper. In this passage, Jesus is about to lay down his life for them, and He gives them final instructions on how to treat each other and demonstrates it in a really beautiful way."

Pages crackle.

"Everyone about there? We'll start in John 13, verse 1, and I'll read through verse 17 in the NIV. It's a long passage so stick with me here: 'It was just before the Passover Festival. Jesus knew that the hour had come for him to leave this world and go to the Father. Having loved his own who were in the world, he loved them to the end. The evening meal was in progress, and the devil had already prompted Judas, the son of Simon Iscariot, to betray Jesus. Jesus knew that the Father had put all things under his power, and that he had come from God and was returning to God; so he got up from the meal, took off his outer clothing, and wrapped a towel around his waist. After that, he poured water into a basin and began to wash his disciples' feet, drying them with the towel that was wrapped around him. He came to Simon Peter, who said to him, "Lord, are you going to wash my feet?" Jesus replied, "You do not realize now what I am doing, but later you will understand." "No," said Peter, "you shall never wash my feet." Jesus answered, "Unless I wash you, you have no part with me." "Then, Lord," Simon Peter replied, "not just my feet but my hands and my head as well!"'"

Some more chuckles.

"Peter's an all-or-nothing kind of guy, isn't he?" Everly says, punctuating the laughter.

"Verse 10," she continues. "'Jesus answered, "Those who have had a bath need only to wash their feet; their whole body is clean. And you are clean, though not every one of you." For he knew who was going to betray him, and that was why he said not everyone was clean.'

"I want to pause right there for a second. Could you imagine being Jesus and washing Judas' feet knowing—*knowing*—this guy is about to betray Him. *That's* love. Anyways, side note . . . sorry, where was I?"

"Verse 12," someone says.

"Thank you. Verse 12: 'When he had finished washing their feet, he put on his clothes and returned to his place. "Do you understand what I have done for you?" he asked them. "You call me 'Teacher' and 'Lord,' and rightly so, for that is what I am. Now that I, your Lord and Teacher, have washed your feet, you also should wash one another's feet. I have set you an example that you should do as I have done for you. Very truly I tell you, no servant is greater than his master, nor is a messenger greater than the one who sent him. Now that you know these things, you will be blessed if you do them.'"

"Wow." Everly pauses, looking at her notes. "That's humbling. Here Jesus, their teacher, their Lord, is washing *their* feet. I could think of a million other things I'd be doing if it was my last moments of life and knew one of these guys was about to betray me. Yet, Jesus took the lead in showing them honor and they were to mimic His example toward one another. Let's pick it up in verse 34: 'A new command I give you: Love one another. As I have loved you, so you must love one another. By this everyone will know that you are my disciples, if you love one another.'"

Everly searches her notes again before looking up at us. "That's how people would know that they were followers of Christ. Love. Not in thought. But in action. And that's how people will know we are Christ followers too, when we choose to live love, despite circumstances.

"God doesn't say loving people is always easy. At times, it can be very tough . . . maybe even the last thing we want to do. Especially when we're more focused on the things people have done to us or said about us, rather than on their identity in Christ. I've really had to wrap my mind around that one lately . . ."

Suddenly, my cheeks are on fire and a trickle of sweat runs down my armpit.

". . . but if Jesus could forgive and love Judas, is there anyone too far gone in our lives where *we* couldn't do the same?"

Please let that include me.

"Remember, being Christian doesn't mean a thing if we're not performing with God's love. God's love is what distinguishes us from common man. We don't separate ourselves. God's love does the separating. It's on a higher level than any other love, and when people see us performing with it on a consistent basis, they just might ask what's different about us. When that happens, that's an open door for us to love them up and share the gospel of Christ with them and maybe save a life. Sound good?"

We nod our heads and Everly closes in prayer.

When Tyler leaves, I start stacking chairs in hopes of having a moment to speak with Everly. Finally, the crowd dwindles, and she's alone stacking chairs, too.

"Hey, Ev."

She continues stacking. "Hey."

"After this can we grab an ice cream and talk?"

Her eyebrows are raised. "You think ice cream's going to win me back?"

"I'm not expecting it to—" I stop stacking. "But it won't hurt. I just want to talk."

"Fine."

When we arrive at Roll 'n Scoop, I continue to give her space as we approach the ice cream counter.

"I'll get my own," she says.

We sit down, and for all I have to say, nothing of substance comes out. "Thanks for your teaching tonight," I manage. "It was healing."

"It was for me too."

"I've missed you, Ev."

"Missed you, too," she responds, ice perhaps slowly melting from her heart. "Thanks for giving me space. This week probably hasn't been easy on you, either."

"I'll wait as long as it takes. Like I said, you're the only one I want."

She throws on a fake smile but her eyes stay put on her ice cream. "Trust is a big thing to me, Jacoby. You had it."

"I'll earn it back. One day at a time. Just give me one more chance. Forgive me, Ev."

"I've already forgiven you. It's the forgetting that's hard. I've had time to think."

Oh, boy.

"I don't think this will be the last time something like this happens, you know?"

"What do you mean?"

"If we continue as 'us'—her fingers make air quotes—"and you keep playing baseball, there will be plenty more girls coming after you. I just don't know if that's something I want to be a part of."

We let that thought settle at the bottom of our empty ice cream cups and scrape it around. "I won't let that happen. Ev, I screwed up. But it made me realize how much you mean to me and how much I want you on this journey with me."

"What do I bring to your life that some other girl can't? I don't own a red bikini."

I let out a sharp laugh. "I'm not laughing at the bikini thing. I'm laughing because I'm still trying to figure out what you see in *me*. You pretty much bring everything to my life."

"Like?"

I try hiding my smile. "Remember that night you were super upset with me about drinking at the hockey game with Bauer?"

Lips pursed, eyes skeptical, she nods.

"Before I ever knocked on your door, I'd already bought tickets and sent them to him, telling him to enjoy the game with someone else."

"You let me rip your head off?"

"Yup."

I miss that laugh.

"But Ev, that's what I'm saying. You saw what was best for me and loved me enough to confront me to my face. Most girls wouldn't care if I went to that game with him and got hammered. But you're not most girls. You see things from a godly perspective. There aren't many like you. None, actually. That I know of, at least."

I grab her hands. "I love you. I've loved you for a long time. I'm not perfect. No one is. But I promise you from here on out I'm going to do everything within me to do right by you."

She smiles, takes a deep breath, and wipes her eyes. "I wanted to be bitter and angry with you all week. And I was. But I started reading about God's love, and it was so healing. I know bitterness, jealousy, and anger are the devil's emotional toys he'd love to wedge between us, so I prayed. I asked God to heal my heart. And yours. I know there will be times when I'll be the one to mess up and you'll have to forgive me."

My glimmer of hope is growing.

"God knows we're dust and fragile," she continues. "He's forgiven me for so much. He's loved me despite knowing every detail of my life. The verses that got me were Ephesians 6:1-2 where we're called to be imitators of God like dear children. If I'm going to imitate my

Heavenly Father who can both forgive *and* forget, I better try to do it, too. I've forgiven you already. And I promise to do my best to forget. So . . . I'm done talking about what happened. I'm not bringing it up again or lording it over your head as ammo. I'm over it. I want you and me—us—to move forward. To use this as an opportunity to grow. Our first bump."

"So . . . a fresh start?"

"Yes. No making it up to me, no trying to be extra whatever. Just be you. The Jacoby I've grown to love. I want to be on this journey together with you. Bringing out the best in each other every step of the way." She takes my hands in hers this time. "Take care of my heart, okay?"

"That's all I want to do."

I walk her to her car. We kiss, and I lift her off the ground, pressing her body firmly against mine. She kisses my forehead then whispers in my ear, "Two are stronger than one. And a threefold chord is not quickly broken. You, me, and God."

After a pause, she declares, "I love you, Jacoby Johnson."

Chapter 21

AT THE END OF April, we wrap up the Orange Empire Conference by beating Riverside and finish with a conference record of 15-6, giving us home-field advantage throughout the playoffs.

Our opening round starts a week from today versus Cuesta, a team from Central Coast California, in a best-of-three series. The winner will move on to a best-of-three Super Regional, followed by a best-of-three Sectional. The final four Sectional winners will meet in Fresno for the double elimination CCCAA Baseball State Championship.

All week at practice, we've been wearing Sarge's orange T-shirts that say, *May Starts with TODAY.*

Coach's Office at Wendell Pickens Field

"Jacoby, come on in," Coach Hill says, waving me into his office. "I thought you should know that a few Major League organizations have been calling about you, lately. I let them know you have a bullpen session today so don't be surprised if you have a few extra eyes out there."

"Are you serious?"

"You've earned the attention. I'm proud of you. Remember, we still have a championship to win, so save some bullets in that arm."

His words, *I'm proud of you*, echo in my mind. I'm floating on my walk back to my car and call Mack.

"Hey Mack, gotta a few minutes?"

"Jacoby, always good to hear from you. I have about five minutes. Everything, okay?"

"Yes. And no. Some high-level scouts are coming to watch my bullpen today."

"And?"

"And . . . My future could be on the line today."

"Jacoby, how many bullpens have you thrown this year?"

"A ton."

"Then why treat this one any different? Is focusing on *the scouts* or the glove going to help you get drafted?"

He's good at shutting me up. "The glove."

"Do you remember what we determined your performance goal would be for the season?"

"Throw one quality pitch at a time."

"So stick with the game plan. It got you this far. When you go to pick up that baseball, treat it like it's the most important pitch of your life, because it is. Let everything else blur into the background. Make them all big pitches—"

"Or all just pitches."

"Exactly. It's just baseball. See your target, breathe, and allow your body to do what you've trained it to do. That's in your control. Whether they call your name in June is up to them."

"Right. I'm just playing catch. Thanks, Mack. I'll let you know how it goes."

I recline on the clubhouse couch, visualizing Coach Jenkins, Branch Calderone, and a few other scouts standing behind the mound as I prepare to pitch from the stretch. I'm comfortable with them there. Not as threats but as admirers. With each pitch, I imagine a smooth release with the ball moving exactly how I want it to move. There's a bucket of balls in each batter's box, one labeled past and the other future. After each pitch the catcher dumps the ball into the past and grabs a new one from the future, tossing it back to me in the present. After my throwing session, I shake each scout's hand and carry on relaxed conversations. *Your turn to shine, Jacoby.*

I open my eyes and the clubhouse is full of chatter about the scouts milling around the bullpen with Coach Jenkins. I head for the outfield grass to loosen up my arm. When I feel good and ready, I play long toss with one of my outfielders. I no longer hear Mack's voice.

Only my own. *Make them all big pitches or all just pitches. You're the best pitcher in baseball. Now, go show them.*

After five minutes of long toss, I head for the bullpen where Coach Jenkins and scouts from the Mariners, Tigers, and Orioles are talking. "Jacoby, come on over here son," Coach Jenkins says. He makes introductions then hands me a baseball. "You ready?"

"Absolutely." I throw about twenty warm-up pitches. The ball is smooth and loose out of my hand, and the plate feels a little closer than usual. Perfect. I signal I'm ready. The scouts are all behind me, just as I visualized, with their radar guns aimed.

Coach Jenkins stands just behind me like he'd done all Fall Ball. "I'll tell you pitch selection and location and you do the rest. Let's start with fastball low and away to a right-hand batter."

Pitching from the stretch, I come set, take a deep breath, and deliver . . .

"Very nice, Jacky boy. Same thing."

After the first pitch, I hit autopilot. No mechanics, no draft, no thinking. Just doing. Being. Allowing my body to do what I've trained it to do.

"That's enough," Coach Jenkins says after around 30 pitches.

I speak to each scout individually for five minutes, the last one being the scout from the Tigers organization, who hold the first overall pick in the draft. We walk towards the warning track in the outfield, and the butterflies that were dormant in the bullpen are waking up.

"Jacoby, I wouldn't be here if I didn't think you had the potential to play professional baseball. Actually, I wouldn't be here if I didn't think you could be pitching in the bigs within two years. That said, if we're going to invest that much money in a guy, we have to do our research. We like to know who we're getting. What kind of person is going to represent our franchise and our city."

"Of course."

"I realize you're coming off a serious injury, but you're young and between your move to the bullpen, the feedback from my associate scouts, and what I just saw, I'm not too worried about your durability. What I do want to address is a video from last fall."

You got to be kidding me. "I can explain everything—"

He puts a hand up. "No need. I talked to your sport psychologist, Marcus Mack."

"You know, Mack?"

"I've been scouting this area for a long time. Mack and I go way back. He's worked with some of the best ballplayers to come out of this area. He didn't share with me too many details, but I understand your parents went through a divorce and you had a moment. I get that. I just want to make sure it's not going to be an issue going forward. As you know, everything's magnified at the next level."

"It's in my past, sir. Like you said, I had a moment but I have a really solid support system in place now. Mack being a big part of it."

"I'm glad to hear that. Is there anything you feel the Tigers should know about you?"

We stop just short of the gate by the outfield fence. "I'm sure you hear this all the time, but it would be an honor to be drafted by the Tigers. I've worked for this my whole life. It got me through physical therapy. When you draft me, you'll never have to worry if I'm all in. I'll give it everything I've got in whatever role the organization sees fit."

"*When* we draft you?" He lets out a huge laugh. "That alone might've earned you a call in a few weeks."

We shake, and he hands me his card before exiting the outfield gate. I do everything to keep my feet on the ground. After practice, I phone Mack again and share with him how well the bullpen session went and thanked him for putting in a good word. We talk strategy for the upcoming last few weeks with everything going on from finals, to the playoffs, to the draft a few weeks away. He reminds me to take a moment to appreciate the entire process.

"You never know what pitch will be the defining pitch in a game," he says. "Strive to win each pitch like it's the game changer. There's no use trying to be perfect. Just think the right thought for the situation. *That's* perfection. Then, take pleasure in those one or two pitches a game that you throw perfectly. That's where the real enjoyment is."

PLAYOFF PICTURE BY THE END OF MAY

In the opening round of the playoffs, we sweep Cuesta College at home in the best-of-three, winning 4-3 and 5-3, respectively. I close out both games without any hiccups.

The following weekend, May 15-16, in the Super Regional, we take down Riverside in two games as well, 2-1 and 11-6. I close out the first game and am not needed for Game 2. On the weekend of May 22-23, we sweep El Camino, 9-0 in Game 1 and 7-4 the next day in Game 2. I close out the second one, recording another save.

In the four games I pitch, I give up just one run. We'd earned our spot to play in Fresno in the Final Four State Championship on the last weekend of May. But I have a lot more than a California state championship on my mind.

My baseball future rides on these next few days. I'm *that* close.

Chapter 22

THURSDAY, MAY 28, 2020, 8:30 A.M.

I'M PACKING FOR FRESNO when Everly knocks at Mack's front door to send me off. She surveys my bedroom from a comfy blue reading chair as I finish packing.

"Where's my hat? I can't find my hat."

"It's right in front of you, babe."

I stuff it in my duffel bag.

"Hey,"—her soft hazels pull me in—"you're going to be great."

"I know. There's just a lot going on right now and I wish you could be there."

"I'm here right now. Just you and me."

Her eyes invite me in, and before my duffel bag hits the carpet,

I'm kissing her. She doesn't fight it. Just giggles. My hands explore her hips, and she bites her lower lip. Her eyes tell me to do whatever I want. Her lack of resistance begs me to show her. I kiss her neck. Her cheek. Her forehead. And finally her lips again. She whispers in my ear. Then bites it gently. I inhale all of her, allowing my hands to explore further.

Ring Ring Ring.

My phone reminder goes off, telling me it's time to leave. *You got to be kidding me.*

I turn it off. "Where were we?"

She whispers in my ear, "You have to go."

"I know, I know. Just one more minute." But the moment's gone. We're both breathing heavy and shaking our heads in frustration. "I can't wait to do that with you every day," I tell her, kissing her one more time.

"Me too."

I zip up my bag, and she walks in front of me to the door. I slide my hand around her waist, not wanting to ever let go. In those few minutes, classroom finals, the State Tournament, and the draft had all disappeared.

FRIDAY, MAY 29, 2020, 2:30 P.M.
Fresno City College, John Euless Ballpark

We open the State Tournament with a season record of 33-14 versus the Sacramento City Panthers, who have a similar season record of 34-14. On a hot dry day, we're ahead 3-1 after five innings, thanks to Sac City's sloppy defense. Our sophomore starter battles through every pitch but is uncharacteristically off and scatters seven hits, three walks and a few hit batsmen, leaving the bases loaded in the 6th before exiting.

We limit the damage, but the Panthers push across two runs to tie it at 3-3 after six innings. In the 7th, Sac City scratches across another run on a sac fly to take the lead, but we answer back in the 8th with Tim's monstrous solo home run.

I enter the game in the 9th inning, tied 4-4. My turn.

The ball has good action out of my hand during warm-ups. The catcher throws down to second after my last toss, and I walk to the back of the mound and face home plate. The batter, a lefty, is announced over the PA system: Cord Shaw.

Just above the hitter, sit a sea of scouts with radar guns trained on me. My future rests on a two-digit reading. Mom sits off the third base line by our dugout, clenching her hands over her mouth. What she's showing on the outside I'm living on the inside. The energy of the crowd pulses through my hand as I grip the laces tight. Sweat is already dripping from my bill in the late afternoon sun.

"Clean inning, Jacky Boy," Coach Jenkins shouts.

The catcher calls for a fastball away. Into the windup, I deliver.

"Ball," the umpire calls.

"Where'd that miss blue?" Coach Jenkins yells.

I get the ball back and toe the rubber. *Who cares? Focus on the next pitch.* The catcher calls for the same pitch. The batter hits it foul down the third baseline, moving the count to 1-1. A fresh ball thuds my glove. The scouts are talking among themselves, probably dissecting my mechanics or pitch movement. The catcher calls for a curveball, which I spike five feet in front of home plate to the moan of the crowd. The count is now 2-1.

We go fastball away again and I miss badly. The count pushes to 3-1. Pitcher's nightmare. Hitter's dream. I miss with a fastball up and away. The hitter swings anyway and laces it right at my third baseman. A loud out. But the hitter and I both know he owned me.

"Settle in there, Jacky boy," Coach Jenkins shouts from the dugout. He has a wad of Big League Chew ready to burst out of his left cheek.

The next hitter doubles in the gap. Then I walk a guy. One out with runners on first and second. *Get it together.*

"Time!" the umpire calls.

Coach Jenkins makes his way from the dugout. "Deep breaths now, son. Deep breaths."

Had I even taken one since the bullpen?

"We jus' fine, okay?" he says. "Ain't nobody hurt. One pitch at a time, son. Stick with your routine. We get you some runs."

He canes his way back to the dugout, and I take in the Fresno air. The scouts are still talking and seem anxious to escape the sun's rays. Mom's slouched deeper in her seat. My insides match her again. I walk the next batter, loading the bases. Then, the unthinkable happens: I walk in a run. *Did you forget how to pitch?*

"Time," the umpire calls.

I peek over my shoulder. Sure enough, Coach Hill walks to the mound and relieves me of my duties, giving me a pat on the butt as I descend the mound. The relief pitcher surrenders another run before we get out of the top of the ninth. We fail to score and lose 6-4.

After the game, we clear out of the dugout for the next two teams to play. In a grassy area behind the field, Coach Hill addresses the team, exploding about our sloppy pitching. Seven walks and four hit batsmen. He reminds us we can't give up free passes and our offense can't fall asleep with a lead.

"We have to step on their necks when they're down," he says. "Get back to the hotel and rest up. Curfew's 10 p.m. tonight. No one believes you can come back from the loser's bracket, but I know it can be done and it starts tomorrow at 10 a.m. Bus leaves at eight."

6:43 P.M.

On the bus ride back to the hotel, my head knocks against the window with the slightest of highway bumps. My eyes shut out the world while I replay the inning. The scouts. The crowd. My mom covering her face. The double. The walks. The draft is slipping away from me, and it's my own doing.

I have dinner with my Mom and Wally. They hit it off while I mostly scrape my food back and forth. After dinner, Wally and I head back to the hotel where I gather my things and let him know I'm staying with my mom in her room so he can get a good night's rest for his morning start. We both know it's unnecessary, but I really just don't want to bog him down with my bad mood.

I turn to leave before he calls to me. "You might go find your toy toilet and flush today's outing."

"Not a bad idea. Might need to flush twice."

9:33 P.M.
La Quinta Inn Lobby

When I turn my phone on to call Everly, a voicemail from a Long Beach area code pops up.

"Jacoby, this is Coach Snell with the Long Beach State Dirtbags. Been keeping tabs on you this year and just watched you pitch tonight. Tough loss. Those nights happen. But I know you can help our program get to Omaha next year. If you don't get what you want in the draft, I hope a full ride can lure you into joining the Dirtbags. Give me a call after Fresno and good luck."

Memories of watching Angels' ace Jered Weaver pitch for Long Beach State filter in. Those wouldn't be bad cleats to follow. Not to mention some leverage in the draft.

I call Everly. Straight to voicemail.

"Hey, pretty lady. Just got my butt handed to me and lost it for us today in front of about 20 scouts. Not great, but I just got a scholarship offer from Long Beach State. I always wanted to go there as a kid. Anyways, I'm staying with Mom tonight and heading to bed early. If we win in the morning, we play tomorrow night. Lose, and I get to see you that much sooner. Hopefully not too soon, though. I love you. Goodnight."

As I get up to leave, Tim and some of the other guys are walking into the hotel. Tim has a backpack slung around his shoulders. I stay seated, hoping they don't see me, but to no avail. The wreak of weed reaches me before their bloodshot eyes do.

"Rough one out there today, Jack," Tim says.

"Tomorrow's another day. Nice home run, though."

"Thanks. I heard the scouts were talking about it."

Oh, I'm sure they were.

"Why don't you come blow off that game with a beer?"

"I already got hammered on the mound today. Once is enough for me."

They laugh. "Your loss. Catch you in the morning."

SATURDAY, MAY 30, 2020, 10 A.M.

The next morning, we're in the visitors' dugout facing off against Mt. SAC, a familiar Orange County foe. We build a comfortable 4-0 lead going into the bottom of the 9th with little drama up to that point, but it's the Final Four and anything can happen. Coach Hill has me warming up just in case things heat up quicker than the Fresno noontime sun.

Sure enough, they do, thanks to two walks and a hit batter to load the bases. Coach Hill and I lock eyes but he doesn't signal for me yet. The next batter laces a three-run double off the center field wall to cut our lead to 4-3, and Coach is kicking himself into a fit. He calls for an intentional walk to make it runners on first and second before signaling me in from the bullpen.

You got this. New day. New moment.

The hitter works the count to 2-2 against me, and on a good pitcher's pitch, he bloops a single over the first baseman's head, bringing in the tying run and moving the winning run 90-feet away on third base. My heart rate ticks up several notches without my permission.

Breathe, Jacoby. Nowhere else you'd rather be. Right guy, right spot.

I run through my routine and on the first pitch, a cut fastball on the outside part of the plate misses the fat part of the bat, resulting in a lazy fly ball to center field. We head to extras. In the dugout, our team is just as shocked as I am at how quickly things went south. I reach into my baseball bag for my mini-toilet, which I flush to remind myself that I made a good pitch on that jam shot and sometimes good pitches get hit.

Coach Hill lets me know I'm going back out for the bottom of the 10th. Two innings of three-up, three-down pitching later, I've given it all I have and I'm lifted for another reliever. My line: 2 innings, one hit, 4 strikeouts, zero walks, and no runs charged to me.

In the 12th, our bats wake up and we pile on six runs to win 10-4, knocking Mt. SAC out of the tournament and presenting us with a chance at redemption versus the Sacramento City Panthers.

In the night game, though, the Panthers end our 14-hour day at exactly midnight, effectively ending our season with an 8-6 victory in which I don't pitch. For us, it was a season in which we started 8-7 overall and saw flashes of greatness, including a 25-6 record to close out the regular season. Our team got back to the State Finals for the third year in a row. Quite an accomplishment. During Coach's final team address, I look around the circle at the sophomores who'd won it all last year and were that close to a repeat. Some of these guys will never play a competitive inning of baseball again. The season may have ended a day short of our goal, but there's plenty to be proud of.

For me personally, I'm hoping there's much more to come with the draft Monday night and Everly by my side.

23

MONDAY, JUNE 1, 2020, 1:15 P.M.

Mack's House

I T'S DAY ONE OF the 2020 Major League Baseball amateur draft. Over the next three days, the top high school and college players in the nation will go from eating Nissin Cup Noodles to cups of caviar, if they're into that sort of thing.

Unfortunately, I'm not hanging out at the MLB Network in Secaucus, New Jersey in a shimmering gray suit, waiting to see if I go in the first two rounds, but, an encouraging text message from Branch Calderone of the Angels says I have a good chance of going on Day Two somewhere between rounds four and 10.

Nineteen years of working toward this moment and the goal I

wrote in that misty mirror on the first day of workouts is on the cusp of becoming reality.

"Babe, you okay?" Everly asks, coming into the living room with a full plate of melted nachos covered in carne asada. "You're looking kind of pale."

I walk to the bathroom mirror and start laughing. "Maybe I *don't* want to watch this. Let's go toss a ball or something."

"What about the range? I've been wanting to break in my new clubs. That's what all pro pitchers do anyway, isn't it? Play golf?"

I poke my head out of the bathroom. "I think they pitch sometimes, too."

I agree that hitting range balls might be a good distraction.

The car ride is silent. Different. Awkward.

Everly cuts into it. "Why am I more excited about today than you? Shouldn't this be the most exciting time in your life?"

"I am excited."

"What's wrong then?"

My eyes stay on the road. "Not sure. Maybe the reality of the whole thing's just hitting me."

"How so?"

"First, it's getting drafted. Then there's life after getting drafted. Competing against the best baseball players in the world."

"And you're about to be one of them." She takes my hand in hers. "Can't you just enjoy the mo—"

"I can't."

A long silence leans in as I turn the wheel into the driving range parking lot. She hasn't heard that tone before.

"Why not?"

Silence.

"Jacoby . . . why not?"

"My dad."

"What about him?"

I put the car in park across from the practice greens, where three older guys are chipping golf balls. "All I've ever wanted is to play pro ball. It started with him in the backyard. He taught me the game. Taught me to love it."

"Then call him."

"Not happening."

"Stop being stubborn and forgive your father. He's *just* a man, remember?"

I crack the windows.

"Don't you think he wants to celebrate with you?"

We look at each other. Her face begins to blur, and I look away. She grips my hand tighter.

"Let's go hit some balls. I'll text him after."

"Call him. Now."

"Ev—"

"Now."

She leaves the car. In the mirror, she grabs our clubs, walks both bags to the ball machine and fills two buckets. My lungs rise and fall as my finger hovers over the call button. I press his number.

Voicemail.

"Hey, Dad. It's me. Was thinking about you today. And lately. A lot." My voice rattles. "I've missed you. I wish you were there to see me pitch this year. I was good. Real good. A scout told me there's a good chance I'll go in the draft tomorrow."

It's the first time I've admitted it out loud.

"We did it, Dad. We did it." I pause. Gather myself. "But it's empty without you. I want you with me tomorrow when I get the call. Let me know if you can meet up at Gallo's for lunch. Love you, Papa."

I rest my head on the steering wheel for several minutes as flashes of T-ball through high school play out on a human highlight reel. The triumphs, the travel, the trophies . . . the fun, the failures, the juice boxes, and the Gatorade. He was always there.

When I climb the driving range stairs to the second deck, Everly has two turf greens staked out side by side with her clubs set up on the farther tee. I drink her in and recall the time I asked Mack how long a Bible teaching should be. His answer was classic. "It should be like a woman's skirt. Long enough to cover the subject but short enough to keep things interesting." Today, Everly's got that mastered.

For the next several minutes, only club face meeting range ball can be heard. She's improved. The thin white stripes on her black tank top hug her torso as she moves gracefully through contact. She never lifts her head. My eyes never leave her.

"Have you been coming out here to practice without me?" I ask.

She turns to me with a blush. "Maybe."

The love of my life. The past six months between us haven't been easy, but we've made sure the bumps have made us stronger.

"You going to hit some balls or just stare?" she says before returning to her own ball. "Your eyes are burning a hole in my backswing."

"Just getting my mind right."

"You better hope so. I'm feeling a win today."

I smooth the turf shavings from the face of my 56-degree wedge. "Your skirt game is a lot better than your short game. I think I'll be alright."

"I don't know what you're talking about, mister."

With my club, I drag a few golf balls onto the turf from the feeder tray. A limp flag 70 yards out calls for a ball. *Eyes down, Jacoby.*

Thwack! We both watch as my ball shanks far right.

"You're definitely losing today," she says. "What are we betting?"

I replace my wedge, walk over, gently cup her face, and pull her lips to mine. I whisper in her ear, "How about a San Diego beachfront house?"

I kiss her again. When I go to pull away, she grabs my elbows tighter toward her. Her eyes soften. "And dessert?"

"Of course," I say, walking backward to change clubs.

"Hey," she says. "Where's my butt tap?"

My girl.

One of the many admirable qualities I love about Everly is her willingness not to pry. No doubt she wants to know about my phone call to my father, but she respects my space enough to let me tell her on my own time. So before we start closest-to-the-pin, I share that I left him a voicemail. Then I take her down, 10-7, even with me giving her a six-shot head start.

"I guess I'm buying us—I mean you—a house in San Diego," she teases. "With the signing bonus *you're* getting, I think we might be able to afford something in New Mexico."

"Oh, you're planning to use *my* money?" I drop my club, sneak up behind her, and bear hug her.

"Don't you know you're my sugar daddy now? Been planning it for months."

"I'll take a house anywhere as long as you'll be there with me." I nuzzle my stubble against her face.

When we finish, I have a text from Dad. *Hey son, I'm at work. Good to hear from you. Gallo's tomorrow at noon?*

TUESDAY, JUNE 2, 2020, 12:04 P.M.

I wait for my dad at Gallo's, our favorite sub shop, watching the crawl on my MLB At Bat app as rounds four, five and six pass by without my name.

My dad walks in. He's a little grayer in the goatee, but happier. Lighter. He hugs me. "You look good, son."

"Good to see you, Dad."

"Shall we order?"

"I already ordered for us. Should be up in a minute. It's on me today."

"Look at you. Becoming a man."

"How've you been?"

"Been good. Real good. The Angels are winning. I'm dating someone. That's *not* married."

"I'm happy for you."

"She's good for me."

"Gotta pic?"

"Sure." He takes out his phone.

"She's got kind eyes."

"She does."

"I've missed you, boy. I caught a few of your games. Couldn't stand not watching you pitch. But never thought I'd see you closing out games."

"You saw me pitch?"

"Yeah, from the outfield. Didn't want to be a distraction. You looked good. Unflappable. Mack did you good."

"You did, too."

Our order comes up and I retrieve it.

He unwraps his sub and takes a bite. "Wasn't sure when I'd hear from you next."

"You can thank my girlfriend."

"Girlfriend? My son? With a girlfriend? All those years and not a single girl at the house. We both move out and now you're sweet on someone?"

I show him the background of my phone. "Her name's Everly."

"She's pretty. What's she like?"

"She's incredible. Loves God. Outgoing, forgiving, encouraging, confronting." My eyes widen. "Very confronting."

"Good. You need that in a woman. Keeps you sharp."

"I've never met anyone like her. Athletic, too. She pushes me to try new things."

"Like seafood?"

"Nah, she gave up on that real quick. But she can get me to try onions here and there if they're cooked just right."

"There's a start. She's not a Dodger fan is she?"

"Angels all the way."

"I like her already," he says, chewing a mouthful of Italian sub. "Things getting serious?"

I swallow my bite, pause, and sip some water. "I know I'm young. And stubborn. But I know what I want and she's it. The last six months with her have been the best of my life, even though they haven't been smooth. But I've got every confidence in God that she's the one. I'm gonna ask her to marry me."

My dad stops mid-bite. "Seriously?"

"Dead serious. I was thinking you and I could go ring shopping after this. I'll have the money to buy something nice with my signing bonus. Her friend borrowed a ring from her to find out her ring size and gave me some suggestions on styles."

His eyes water. Mine follow suit. I've missed him. He stands and hugs me for a long time. "I'm happy for you son. Congratulations."

"She still has to say yes."

We sit back down and resume our meal.

"What style ring does she like?"

"Nothing big. She's not flashy. I love that about her."

"Your mother was the same way. Never needed me to prove my love to her with a huge rock despite what these Orange County women lug around. I swear they all have back problems because of it. So, when are you planning to propose?"

"I'm thinking next week sometime. Mom wants to throw me a draft party when things settle down. Probably then. It'll be our six-month anniversary."

"Does your mother know?"

"You're the first I've told."

He beams with pride, nods slightly, and wads up his wrapper. "I'd be honored to help you pick out a ring, son. I'd also like to pay for half."

"Then I'm getting the biggest rock I can find." I'm unable to keep a straight face. "Seriously, though Pops. You don't have to."

"I want to and I am. My son's getting married. I'd like to meet her."

"She wants to meet you, too."

He leans to the side, looking behind me. "What's that you've been hiding?"

"This." I hand him a wrapped frame. "It's for you."

He unwraps it like a three-year-old at Chuck E. Cheese's. A fogged-in Golden Gate Bridge reflects in his eyes as he reads line by line. Since living at Mack's house, I've taken to the poems scattered throughout the house.

"This is really something, son."

"Read it out loud." I close my eyes. "It's my favorite."

"Okay. It's called 'The Bridge Builder' by Will Allen Dromgoole . . .

> *An old man going a lone highway,*
> *Came, at the evening cold and gray,*
> *To a chasm vast and deep and wide,*
> *Through which was flowing a sullen tide.*
> *The old man crossed in the twilight dim;*
> *The sullen stream had no fear for him;*
> *But he turned when safe on the other side,*
> *And built a bridge to span the tide.*
>
> *"Old man," said a fellow pilgrim near,*
> *"You are wasting your strength with building here;*
> *Your journey will end with the ending day;*
> *You never again will pass this way;*
> *You've crossed the chasm, deep and wide,*
> *Why build this bridge at even tide?"*
>
> *The builder lifted his old gray head.*
> *"Good friend, in the path I have come," he said,*
> *"There followed after me today*
> *A youth whose feet must pass this way.*
> *This chasm which has been as naught to me,*
> *To that fair-haired youth may a pitfall be;*
> *He, too, must cross in the twilight dim:*
> *Good friend, I am building this bridge for him."*

I slowly let the restaurant music and chatter back in.

"I love it, son."

"Good. It holds a special significance. That night—at your place—I hated you. Over the next few months, I bottled it up and made some bad decisions. Things I'm not proud of."

His joy turns to wrinkles. "Why didn't you ever call me?"

"You were why I started it all in the first place. Then when I found out I was moved to the bullpen, it was a kind of breaking point for me. And that's the day I found your letter. Now, every time I read this poem, I see you fighting against the tide, building that bridge for me. Your letter was that bridge. It showed me a better, easier path to walk." I study my sub wrapper. "I wasn't sure I'd ever share that with you."

His eyes wander back. "I wish I could've been there for you."

"You were. Your words were. That was enough. So thank you. Your words showed me what not to do."

"I wish I could've been a better example of what *to* do. My actions cost me everything. You don't think about any of that at the time. I'm sorry, son. I'm sorry for all of it. I failed you."

Silence sits between us.

"I forgave you a long time ago," I tell him. "For everything. Everly helped me with that. She said, 'God's not holding it against him, so why should you?'"

"Sounds like a wise girl. This poem means the world to me, Jacoby. I'll be your bridge builder any day."

I move across the booth and bury my head in his shoulder, the one he'd thrown thousands of batting practice balls to me with. "Love you, Papa."

"I love you, son."

My choo-choo train whistles.

"It's the Angels scout." My eyes dart back and forth trying to comprehend what I'm reading. "I just went in the 7th round!"

My tears soak into his shirt. Nineteen years of ups and downs, setbacks and comebacks all summed up in this one text: *7th round. Welcome to the Angels.* When I lift my face, several other Gallo's patrons are staring.

Dad looks at me, beaming.

"What do you say you and I go find your Everly a ring?"

Chapter 24

SATURDAY, JUNE 6, 2020

MUCH OCCURRED IN THE days following the draft. I took meetings with three different sports agencies vying to represent me and negotiate my contract. Mack had given me criteria to consider going into each meeting including: culture, fit, integrity, facilities, endorsement opportunities, and quality of players currently represented. Mack warned me this wasn't something to take lightly.

I ended up going against conventional wisdom and signed with the smallest of the three agencies. Simply put, PSI Sports Management in Ventura, California, felt like home. Don't get me wrong, they currently represent some of the top Major Leaguers and have a ton of rising stars about to break through to the bigs, but you wouldn't know it by how the staff carried themselves. They weren't flashy. They were real.

When I walked into headquarters, I was met by Jeremy Turner, the head agent. He could've been the receptionist for all I knew. Humble, straightforward, and carried a quiet confidence that told me he'd fight just as hard for an extra five dollars on my monthly minor league salary as he would negotiating a $5 million endorsement deal with Under Armour.

He showed me around the facility, starting in the players' lounge. Big-screen TVs with video games and MLB Network on the wall. Protein powder cases and mini fridges stocked with water bottles. "Just keeping it real," he told me.

Apparently, every January the minor leaguers, and even some Major Leaguers, participate in an eight-week pre-spring training workout program to prepare for the grueling season ahead. In the hallways leading from the players' lounge to the gym were more pictures and framed jerseys of Major League clients with #Roadtothe-Show stickers on the glass. The gym was expansive and conveniently featured batting cages and pitcher's mounds for guys to get their work in all in one place without any distractions, before relaxing or playing Spike Ball at one of the rented beach houses.

The head athletic trainer was in house the day I visited. Afterwards, Jeremy warned me, "He plays nice guy right now. But when you show up for winter workouts, you already better be in good shape. He'll make you throw up or cry. Sometimes both. But you'll still be pitching well into the dog days of summer when everyone else is breaking down. We believe in his process as much as he believes in us to bring in quality guys. We're family here."

When it came to my signing bonus, Jeremy didn't disappoint. He was able to negotiate a $220,001 signing bonus. That was $15,000 above slot value. More than enough for a nice engagement ring for my Everly. I also bet him a dollar he couldn't negotiate me the extra dollar. He got it for me. Not bad for a 7th round junior college player with a surgically repaired throwing arm.

Two days before my draft party, the water heater burst at Mom's house, jeopardizing everything. In a last-ditch effort, I called Mack and asked if he'd allow me to host the party at his house. He was in the hospital with Suzanne's mother and couldn't talk long but told me he was proud of me, disappointed he wouldn't be able to make it, and that, of course, we could host the celebration party at his house. Mom and Everly went to work. My only responsibility was the guest list.

The list began with my first Little League coach, Mike Miller. He taught me how to win. It seems obvious that a coach would do that, but in my first two years of Little League, I was the Derek Jeter of the league and basically won everything possible. To this day, I've never tolerated losing for long.

Next I thought of my travel ball coaches and team moms for both basketball and baseball. Winning was important to them, too, but it was their generous investments of time, energy, and money into my athletic development that I remember most. They paid for hotels and tournament fees. They picked me up and dropped me off for practices and games when my parents couldn't swing it. I didn't appreciate or even grasp the investment they put into my life at the time. Of course they were invited.

High school was helpful for two reasons. We weren't great my junior and senior seasons, so it's where I developed a stronger appreciation for winning and a deep-seated hate for losing. A moment in my freshman year on JV stands out. Coach Sanchez was livid when a few guys slacked big time on fundraising. After an hour of running sprints, we played fungomania and he was hitting fungoes with exit velocities ranking *super angry* on the choppy JV field. Coach said seven words to me that day that are tattooed in my memory: "Don't let me hit it by you." I've never forgotten that. It wasn't a demand. It was a mentality. He was invited.

Then, of course, there was the surgery that changed my career path or at least sent me on a detour for a couple years. After scouts shied away from drafting me out of high school and my scholarship was revoked, I would've been all but lost if it hadn't been for Mack. He saved my career. He'll be missed at the party.

There were a few who wouldn't make it on my invite list, although each one taught me lessons that will pay off down the road. Guys like my shortstop Tim Fletcher, who taught me what kind of lifestyle I don't want to be involved in. Plus he almost broke my face.

Shawn Bauer taught me that having it "all" by the world's standards is not all that it's cracked up to be. The girls, the booze—all of it—is empty and counterfeit. Flashy and tempting? Sure. I'd be lying if I said I didn't have fun. But that kind of fun carried plenty of consequences that could have been easily avoided.

Then there's Fallon. She taught me that looks almost kill. Like an ox headed for slaughter, I followed her down some dark paths and paid for it. More than once. But like Everly said, there's a Fallon around every corner whispering, calling your name, and enticing you to her bed.

Back on the positive side, Coach Hill taught me nothing is guaranteed in baseball or in life. The world owes you nothing. Every day's a one-day contract and you have to earn the next one. It took me seeing how good a pitcher Tyler was to understand Coach's goal of giving the team the best chance to win. And I have to thank him for giving me a new love for the bullpen. I want Coach Hill there along with Coach Jenkins and Sarge, of course.

I was stoked to hear that Tyler Waltrip got drafted, too, in the 10th round by the Miami Marlins. Even better, we're brothers in Christ now because he invited Jesus Christ into his life—lengthening his rope to eternity.

Mack's house

Guests arrive as the sun is still above the horizon. The backyard lattice is lit up with strands of dangling lights above the refreshments table. There's no beer, which I'm sure will disappoint a bunch of my old teammates.

After mingling for a while, I escape to the guest bathroom. Six months ago, I made a commitment to do things the right way, and for the most part I had. Now, that kid had grown up. Somewhat. My stomach expands and deflates as I trace the outside of a small red felt box in my pocket. My watch flashes 113 bpm.

A knock comes at the bathroom door, pushing it slightly ajar.

"Mack! What are you? I mean . . . wow! You're here."

We embrace, and the memories of all we've been through to get here flood in. The in-person sessions, the phone calls, the tough conversations, living in his house, the mental game goodies—all of it. He tells me Suzanne's mother had passed away in her sleep three days ago. I hug him again, give my condolences, and tell him what I am about to do. "Any final words of wisdom?"

"Never stop dating her. Treat her special." He taps my chest. "Speak from here. And breathe. A lot."

We return to the party, and Everly is gleaming in a small gathering across the way. She's above and beyond what I could ask or think. God's realm of specialty. And it's just the beginning. I tap a water glass with a fork and ask for the floor. Heads turn and the backyard quiets.

"I want to thank everyone for being here tonight. Although this party is supposed to be for me, it's really for all of you. Without each of you playing a huge role in my life, I wouldn't be standing here. I've got coaches here from Little League all the way up to Coach Hill, Coach Jenkins, and Sarge over there. I'm thankful to each one of you for the role you've played in my career. Whether it was a word of encouragement, a ride home, the truth, or a fist," —some laughs come from the baseball guys— "each of you forced me to stretch my comfort zone and take my game up a notch. Thank you."

I point to Sarge. "Nine months ago, I stood next to that man in a circle similar to this one, surrounded by a group of angry teammates. I had failed them by dropping my 'girlfriend' —as Sarge likes to call his 45-pound plates—before time was up and the team almost had to repeat the whole thing. Fortunately for me, Sarge didn't have them go through with it."

Sarge's Crest white teeth are visible in the low light.

"After the workout, I asked Sarge why he calls those 45-pound plates 'girlfriends.' Do you remember what you told me?"

"They have the power to break you down or build you up," he says, as people share a light chuckle.

"That day I was humbled by that cement plate and many times throughout Fall Ball."

I pivot to Everly. "But then I started hanging out with this girl who showed me the other side of Sarge's comment. The building-up side. Everly, you've absolutely been a rock for me over the past six months. Can you come up here, please?"

Everyone makes room for her, allowing me to take a final deep breath. Her flowing white summer dress and weathered brown cowboy boots are accompanied by a bewildered grin.

"If you haven't met her already, this is Everly—the most important woman in my life besides that incredible woman right over there"—I point to my mom. "Can we give them a round of applause for putting all this together."

My stomach fills with air as I take Everly's hands in mine. "Everly Stevens. I remember the first time I saw you last year at campus ministry. I pretty much kept going because of you."

Laughter and tears well up in her.

"Then, this year, in that first meeting at G2G when you ended your conversation to come say hi and sat next to me . . . I loved that. Then you scared the crap out of me when you started teaching God's

Word. Your heart for God is golden. You know His Word. But, more importantly, you *do* His Word. You live it. I've learned that difference from you. You know I'm far from perfect. In our six months together, you've had every opportunity to walk away every time you've seen me stumble. You know my faults. You see them all, yet you choose to see less."

A tear streaks down her cheek.

"A wise man once told me the greatest thing we can do in a relationship is to love God more than we love each other. It gives each person the freedom to not have to be perfect. The freedom to make mistakes. It gives each person the right to rely on God's limitless ability to provide rather than on a partner's limited supply. It allows us to be our best. You've demonstrated that to me, and I promise to always love God more than I'll ever love you. I know at some point I'll let you down. But I also know that God never will. *You* are what I want in this life, and God's blessed me bigger than I could've ever imagined."

I pull the red felt box from my pocket and take a knee, stealing a breath. Everly's hands cover her mouth.

"Everly Stevens, will you marry me?"

With wide eyes, she shakes her head up and down. "Yes. Yes, of course, I will."

I slide the ring on, unable to erase the smile from my face. The ring is even more elegant on her hand. I press my lips to hers, and the clapping fades into the background. It's just us and God.

10:33 P.M.

Hours later, when everyone has left except for Mack, Everly, and my mom, Mack asks for a moment alone with me in his office. He flicks the light on, and the room sparkles. We tour his sanctuary like it's the first time. I smile, knowing the vacant spot on the wall will soon be filled. We sit down across from each other.

"I'm really proud of you, Jacoby."

His words wash over me.

"I couldn't have done it without you."

I tell him about meeting up with Dad.

His forearms lean into the desk. "That's great to hear you're reconciling with your father. It's a heavy burden to be able to drop, I'm sure. Listen, in a few weeks here you'll be heading out for pro ball. The next level is still just baseball. Sure, there are more fans, more cameras, and you're making some money now, but it's the same game and you've got the same God. There'll be a whole new set of pressures and pleasures you haven't faced yet. Plenty of triumphs, too. Embrace it all. Stick to your routines. Read your Bible every day. Remember who you are in Christ and never budge. Practice God's presence on a moment-by-moment basis. And go out and perform with the love of God on and off—"

"Wait a minute." Several campus ministry meetings flash through my mind. "That's what Everly's been sharing . . . wait. Are you—?"

He can't hold back his smile any longer. "I was wondering when you would figure it out."

"You mean to tell me the blonde sitting next to you at the funeral was Everly?"

"It was. Everly's my granddaughter."

My world is swirling. "Why didn't you ever tell me? Why didn't she tell me?"

"I'm a lockbox remember? She takes after me. You did well, Jacoby. She's . . . well, she's the best."

"She is, isn't she?"

"Love her up. Make her your queen, and she'll treat you like her king. Marriage is the most beautiful relationship God designed. In the tough times ahead, remember that Everly is first and foremost your sister in Christ and then your wife. Choose to see that first. Then in everything you do, separate her from all other women. Elevate her to the next level. To higher ground."

GROUP DISCUSSION

GROUP DISCUSSION QUESTIONS AND SELF-STUDY

1. What evidence in the early chapters demonstrates Jacoby's commitment to getting drafted in June 2020?

2. After Jacoby's first outing in Fall Ball, he and Mack discuss how emotional green, yellow, and red lights positively or negatively impact **body language, focus, and self-talk.** Write out your own green, yellows, and reds, (situations they occur, and how they impact the three categories above). Share with your accountability partner(s) and discuss routines for getting back to green.

3. Proverbs 25:28 NIV says, *"Like a city whose walls are broken through is a person who lacks self-control."* After dinner with his Dad on Halloween weekend, what do Jacoby's emotions drive him to do? What pitfalls lead to his downfall? Could this happen to anyone, no matter how committed they are to their goals?

4. Think of people in your own life who may be similar to the following characters: Tim, Bauer, Fallon, Everly, Mack, and Wally. How are the people you invest time with helping or hurting you towards your best self and athletic goals? Who might you spend less time with? Invest more time with?

5. Why might Fallon and Jessica (in the red bikini) have been so willing to throw themselves at Jacoby? What can you learn from Jacoby's choices with these girls and the aftermath of his choices? How will you handle similar situations?

6. After reading the letter from his dad, what does Jacoby learn about the dangers of pornography?

7. How does Everly impact Jacoby's life? Describe 2-3 specific instances.

8. What qualities/characteristics will you begin looking for in a significant other?

9. What qualities/characteristics in a significant other will you be more cautious about?

10. Even though Jacoby knows the mental game, what situations still seem to trip him up and get him away from his performance routines (breathing, positive self-talk, strong body language)? Looking at your own performance, what situations or people tend to get you off your game? How might you remedy this?

11. Proverbs 31:10 NIV says, *"A wife of noble character who can find? She is worth far more than rubies."* At the end of the book, Jacoby (age 20) proposes to Everly. Do you agree with his decision? How might this be helpful for him? What problems do you foresee, if any?

12. Near the end of the story, Jacoby finally forgives his father, despite the ripple effects his dad's decisions had on Jacoby's entire world. What do you think motivated Jacoby to forgive his father? What was the outcome between father and son? Is there anyone in your life you need to forgive and reconcile with? Or forgive, at the very least? What might the outcome be?

13. What were your biggest takeaways from Jacoby's journey to pro baseball? What were the events that cost *him* big time, that, if you learn from his mistakes, will help you bypass the pitfalls he experienced?

In what way did *Playing on Higher Ground* impact you the most? It would bless me big time if you shared it on Amazon in a review!

Haven't read the beginning of Jacoby's Journey? Get it on Amazon, today!

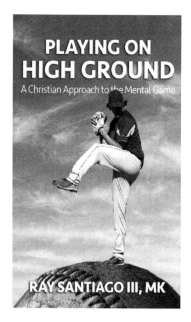

Do you have a Mack in your life?
If not, work with Ray!
Email: Ray3@RenewedMindPerformance.com

Ready to elevate your mental game in 21 hours?
www.RenewedMindPerformance.com/21hmp

CONNECT WITH RAY ON SOCIAL MEDIA

RenewedMindPerformance

RenewedMindRay3

RenewedMindPerformance

Made in the USA
Lexington, KY
13 December 2019